SEA RHAPSODY

Sea Rhapsody

A Novel

by

Joan Davies

GEE AND SON LIMITED
DENBIGH

ISBN 0 7074 0152 6

All characters in this novel are entirely fictitious and have no reference to any living person.

Printed and Published by

GEE & SON LIMITED, DENBIGH, CLWYD, WALES

Chapter 1

The young violinist re-entered for the third time to take his encore. Thick black curls fell attractively over his pale face as he bowed to his captivated audience. When their enthusiastic applause had died down, he faced the rows of excited music-lovers to announce his fourth solo.

'Thank you very much, ladies and gentlemen, for the wonderful welcome you have given me tonight. For my final solo I will play one of my favourite pieces, Dvorak's *Humoreske*.'

Once more, to complete silence, the young man wielded his bow expertly over the strings, producing a golden tone rarely heard among string players. As he played there was something un-canny about the atmosphere. Every eye was upon him, every ear responsive to the brilliance of his performance. He bowed several times before leaving the stage and finally the musical director was forced to subdue the loud and prolonged clapping in order to continue the evening's programme.

Elizabeth had an excellent view from her usual front row seat. Here, she had realised at once, was a violin player of the utmost distinction. He handled his instrument in such a way that it spoke forth his whole soul to his spell-bound audience.

'No doubt about it, he's an absolute genius.'

Eyes sparkling, voice full of excitement, Elizabeth had approached Dr. Peter Emmanual during the coffee interval.

'Do tell me where you discovered this little virtuoso for our Palm Court Orchestra.'

The doctor smiled happily at her and sipped his coffee. Re-placing his cup and saucer on the table, he produced a small red diary from his inside pocket and turned the pages.

He looked every inch the proud professor, this tall, broad should-

5

ered, over-weight man with impressive features and a thatch of greying black hair. Everything about him suggested strength and authority, but especially the appealing brown eyes, the kind of eyes which spoke for themselves and forced others to do his bidding. His movements suggested strength of character, his dignified air enhanced by the cut of his Saville Row suit, fancy shirt, purple bow tie and black patent shoes.

'No credit to me, Liz, I make no secret of that,' he said. 'But I do keep my ear to the ground where talent is concerned. I came across this young man in his final year at the college of music, and, after hearing his slow movement from the Tchaikovsky concerto, I was determined to get him here for the season. Solos such as we have heard tonight will, I conjecture, draw the crowds back to the pier head pavilion like bees round a honey pot . . . Ah yes, here we are: I did make a note of it. Giovanni Malvolio, aged nineteen, Manchester College of Music.'

The doctor replaced the diary and picked up his coffee cup.

'My congratulations upon your choice, Doctor! He has such control of his bow. Never have I heard that Allegro played at such a pace . . . And still so young.'

Their eyes met and, with an understanding smile, Elizabeth patted the professor's shoulder.

The general conversation in the coffee bar was centred round the same theme. People queued up for their coffee, then seated themselves at the white tables and chairs along the pleasant sun lounge — the mighty ocean spread out beneath them. The doctor was beaming: clearly he thoroughly enjoyed his reflected glory.

'What worries me at this moment, Liz, is that I've brought him here for our first concert of the season and, as yet, found no accommodation for him. He'll need encouragement and a quiet place to practise.'

Dr. Emmanual could be charm itself. Eyes alight, he gave Elizabeth one of his most brilliant smiles and squeezed her hand.

'I wonder, my dear — could you take him off my hands?'

The doctor felt he was on safe ground. Most of her spare time, he knew, was devoted either to playing or to listening to classical music, so what hardship would it be to her to have a young virtuoso player around the house?

Elizabeth's mind did a somersault as a surge of maternal instinct swept through her veins. To get that boy into her home — what bliss! But could a busy guest house be the right environ-

6

ment? All the guest rooms were taken, leaving only Roger's room, and he was away.

Impulsively she said, 'Very well, Peter, I'll take him. How could I resist such an opportunity? He'll have my husband's room. Roger is always away at this time of year.'

'But of course. Some sort of electrical engineer, is he not, and now in Arabia?'

'That's it. Saudi Arabia to be exact, near Jedda.'

'And how is he faring?'

'He loves being away.' Her tone evasive, Elizabeth took care to avoid the doctor's quizzical gaze. 'He gets a kick out of the climate out there, likes the people too. And his work has the same appeal for him that music has for me.'

'But he does come home sometimes, I take it, and you are both happy with the arrangement?'

Elizabeth fumbled about in her handbag for a handkerchief.

'We jog along, you know, going our separate ways. Not much love lost. Suits us both. As long as he keeps out of the way of my music, it's O.K. with me.'

There was a certain bitterness in her voice. Her eyes clouding over, she did her best to hide the tears which escaped and flowed freely down her smooth pink cheeks. Managing a watery smile, she nodded to the doctor and started to make her way back to the concert.

'So that's settled — good,' he called after her. 'You know, Liz, I'm more than relieved about this. You've done me a great favour. He has no home, no parents and very few belongings at all.'

In an attempt to avoid looking conspicuous, Giovanni had carried his coffee along to the dressing room to enjoy it in a quiet corner behind a stack of music folios. A minute later Les came breezing along, almost knocking him over in his hurry to find a piece of music; he had not expected to find Giovanni's timid form crouching in the shadows.

'Why, I nearly walked right through you. Welcome to the orchestra, Giovanni! Hope I didn't hurt you?'

Les sounded jovial and his tone was encouraging. He'd been playing that grand piano for a number of years and was almost part of the furniture.

'No, that's all right. But I wonder — would you help me out a bit? This is my first summer season,' Giovanni ventured, 'and

7

I don't want to start off by dropping clangers.' He sounded unsure of himself, an appealing look in his dark eyes.

'Why, of course, kid,' was Les' ready response. 'Jolly being at a seaside resort, y'know, and the atmosphere in the orchestra is quite relaxed — not like playing in the Hallé! Anyway, if you have any problem at all don't hesitate to come to me. See you!'

Giovanni was gratified at the welcome on Les's face. He was wondering frantically about his digs for the season. Doctor Emmanual had mentioned a lady who would probably take him — a regular concert goer, keen on classical music. He must make a good impression. He did so hope people would like him. He would much prefer to have a room of his own: the thought of having to share, or of being one of a crowd was anathema to him. He knew his playing was O.K., but felt secretly dissatisfied with his inability to mix. As it was, a quiet guest house sounded the very thing, as well as a motherly person to take him on.

What would it be like living in Wales, he wondered? Was it really a land of song? He knew Welsh Choirs were famous for their zeal and enthusiasm, but he had yet to come across a good instrumentalist from Wales. It would be pleasant to get some sea air into his lungs, and he must climb Snowdon and cross the famous Menai Bridge to Anglesey.

Leader of the Youth Orchestra for two years, he had played in many a college concert but had yet to gain experience of a real concert orchestra in a famous seaside resort for the whole summer season. Anyway, Dr. Emmanual had chosen him out of all the students and been kind enough to bolster his confidence. Here indeed was a challenge: his first professional job. A member of the musicians' union at last, he would be handling his own money for the first time.

The second half of the concert passed all too quickly. From her favourite seat, Elizabeth had a splendid view of all sixteen instrumentalists, and, the one sad moment having passed, she could return to her dream world. of music. The season-ticket tucked away in her handbag entitled her to attend every concert from the middle of April right through to the end of September, with one round of glorious music from the classics.

Swallow Tree Gardens was set on a hill overlooking the expansive bay of a select seaside resort in North Wales, only three minutes' walk from the pier gates. Elizabeth aimed at accommodating from twelve to fifteen guests for twenty weeks and thus making herself independent of her husband. Roger could live his life and she could run hers. He had made it clear that he could not stand the continual music which invaded the house, but that had not made the slightest difference to Elizabeth. Music was her life and always would be.

It didn't matter how strenuous was her work of catering for these hungry guests, or how difficult the elderly visitors could be, her determination did not flinch. Problems with tradesmen, cancellations or double bookings never worried her. The guest house was there to make money: secondary in her life. If dried carrots were easier to prepare and ready-made pastry-mix quicker to get on to the dinner tables, then convenience food it was. Nothing, she had resolved, should prevent her from attending her beloved evening concerts.

There was no escaping the determination in Elizabeth's corn-flower blue eyes — and yet, at times, those same penetrating eyes could display a wealth of compassion and sympathy. Soft hair, almost blonde, framed a healthy open air face to give her an out-door appearance, equally borne out by the fact that, no matter what the weather, her trim figure could be seen striding the Welsh hills in jeans and jumper, woollen hat and gloves, her face set in a serious expression as she worked out her latest plans and designs for her own or somebody else's future.

Elizabeth rarely sought advice, nor confided, even to Roger, whom she held in the palm of her hand. He would conform all right, she assumed, and be the first to congratulate her at the end of the struggle. More at home in the company of intellectuals of either sex, she experienced far more thrills and passionate emotion from the Beethoven Symphonies than from anything Roger could offer.

Just as efficiently as she handled staff and guests alike in her homely seaside guest house, so she could have managed the catering arrangements for a six month cruise on the Q.E.2. To organise an Albert Hall concert, complete with top stars, would have been a piece of cake to Elizabeth, who would have seen it through unhesitatingly, and with undoubted success. Then she would happily have slunk away into the shadows, expecting neither praise nor reward.

Like an express train hurtling through all stations, she pursued her ideals regardless of setbacks until her objectives were achieved. There was a certain courage there, which was inexplicable. Elizabeth's desire to be admired and loved could be disturbing and, at times, had led her into trouble. There was a tinge of possessiveness and jealousy in her nature which occasionally reared its head to cause trouble all round, and when really wounded she found it very, very hard to forgive.

Gretta, the German au-pair girl, had fitted in very well. This capable sixteen year old could safely be left in charge to clear away the evening meal and serve coffee in the lounge, while Elizabeth grabbed coat, gloves and handbag at precisely the same time each evening.

Tonight was Saturday, arrival day. 'There's just one couple not yet arrived, Gretta dear,' Elizabeth explained. 'Show them Room Ten and let them help themselves to the cold meat and salad. You'll find plenty of trifle on the trolley with the cheese and biscuits. Bye — see you around ten. Auf Wiedersehn.'

What paradise it was to walk that quarter mile of the pier, she reflected, watching the pink clouds moving overhead as the sun began to set over the bay. What a superb month was April for freshness! The tangy smell of seaweed mingling with the salty air was tonic in itself as she felt the spray on her face and tasted the salt from the sea. The screeching of herring gulls overhead was music in her ears as they pounced greedily on any scraps of food left behind by the visitors. As she hurried along the pier, Elizabeth could hear the waves beating vigorously against the iron structure beneath her and breaking on the pebbly shore further on. The pleasant sea breeze whipped colour into her cheeks as she passed the newly painted kiosks attracting holidaymakers to buy souvenirs, tee shirts and candy.

At the end of the concert, Elizabeth remained in her seat as the crowd streamed out into the cool night air. As the double doors opened she was aware of a pleasant breeze and a few stray seagulls flying noisily towards their nests in the over-hanging cliffs. Then there was the usual clunk clunk, like drums, of several hundred feet making their way along the wooden slats of the pier.

It would be at least ten minutes before Dr. Emmanual got away from behind that stage to introduce her to Giovanni, so she must be content to wait in her seat. Her thoughts were racing. This would be the first time she had ever played host to a real musician under her roof. Would she be able to pick his mind and get to know all the inner mysteries of the musical world? Might he help her along with her piano playing and those songs she had composed?

The pavilion was strangely quiet after the hubbub and chatter of the crowd. Conversations had ceased, the lights had dimmed, and the last few stragglers were making for the exit. Beyond that red velvet curtain those sixteen members of her favourite orchestra would be packing away their instruments, and one of them was going to be hers, to cherish, to mother and to indulge. Yes, he was there back stage, with Peter, no doubt, full of praise for his performance and advising him about his digs. Oh, why were they taking so long? The front row seat seemed increasingly hard and uncomfortable!

Suddenly, out of the blue, Elizabeth's friend Naomi appeared and sat down beside her.

'I've been looking for you, Liz. My dear, what a successful first night,' she gushed. 'I did enjoy it so terribly. Wasn't the perform-ance of our little player quite splendid? But darling,' she rattled on, 'you look positively overcome. No cause for tears on such a night. I couldn't help noticing them in the interval as you chatted to Dr. Emmanual. Do tell me what's on your mind.'

The two women, though good friends, were not a bit alike. Elizabeth admired Naomi more for her refinement and discrim-ination than for anything else. Her glossy auburn hair hung back from a flawless delicately sculptured face, her make-up immaculate, her slender rose-tipped fingers sparkling with diamonds. Slim and shapely, she wore tonight a cream linen suit which emphasised her golden tan.

A pleasant mouth had Naomi and brown eyes that seemed to dance with amusement. As she turned her head, her hair cascaded over her shoulders in highlights of red and gold. Three rows of pearls with matching ear rings added a sparkle of sophistication. She was a city lady and always would be. The holiday flats had been her husband's idea, Elizabeth knew, and she had gone along with his desire to get out of the rat race and into the fresh air.

Naomi's swift perfumed embrace brought Elizabeth out of her daydream.

'It's nothing really,' she said. 'Take no notice of me, I'm just being silly . . .'

Her tone was far from assuring and before long she was confiding to her friend:

11

'Dr. Emmanual has persuaded me to take the little violin player for the season. Well, you know, as I watched his face on that stage tonight I saw my own little son all over again.' Her lips quivered and a sob entered her voice: 'It was those black curls and that small oval face — so pale and sweet. That — that's what Timothy would have been like.'

'The little boy you lost . . .' Naomi took her hand and squeezed it gently.

Would she ever forget that dreadful day five years ago? Though she hated to bring it back it often loomed up in her thoughts.

It had been one of those frustrating Saturday mornings, work piling up all round, guests coming and going, the usual change-over. She had suggested that Roger take Timothy with bucket and spade down to the beach while she collected the dirty linen upstairs.

Four year old Tim, it seemed, had played with his dad on the sands until one of Roger's pals had turned up and talked him into a quick drink at the Marine Hotel. Elizabeth never understood the stupidity of leaving such a young child alone. Intent upon his sand castle with turrets and a moat, he would not have missed his father at first. So the short drink had become a long one, and Roger hadn't recognised the danger that Tim might walk into the water to fill his bucket and, in his enthusiasm, go deeper and deeper into the sea; the danger of a wave coming along to envelop his tiny figure and, half an hour later, of the poor child being found, floating head downwards in the sea, his bucket and boat several yards away.

Elizabeth well remembered with what heartache she had sat in that hospital corridor. All the resuscitation equipment in the world could not save the child she had doted on for four whole years, whose lungs had become saturated with salt water.

In her torment she had blamed Roger bitterly for what she regarded as his gross negligence, and that was how the rift had started in their marriage: she couldn't bring herself to forgive him. Instead she had buried herself in her music, sometimes playing concertos into the small hours, and Roger had opted out by fixing himself up with this electrical engineering post in Saudi Arabia, where he spent most of the year.

Elizabeth blew her nose, mopping each eye with her tiny hankie. Naomi, who knew all about it, registered nothing but kindly sympathy:

'You've been extremely brave, my dear, and now you're going to be brave again. You've agreed to take on this violin player without parents or home. You'll get all the music you need and have someone depending on you again. I shouldn't wonder if you find him taking the place of little Timothy all over again.'

Giovanni dusted his violin and packed it lovingly into its velvet lined case. As he screwed down his bow, his one wish was for a better instrument — one that would 'speak' more eloquently for him.

Backstage everybody was racing about, grabbing at instruments, shouting, laughing, joking, and then rushing off in pairs. Why did he lack their sense of humour and ability to make conversation? Soon he was left in the dim shadows of the stage, with the silk purple curtain stretching above him.

He knew Dr. Emmanual was still occupied with paperwork in that glass-partitioned office place where everything seemed to happen. Someone was switching off the lights in the main hall and all had gone deathly quiet, so he must just wait in this little alcove till the doctor was ready.

He was going to meet that lady. She must be the one in the neat brown suit, with flowing fair hair, who had clapped like mad and cheered him on from her front row seat. She looked a lot younger than Matron.

'There I go,' he murmured. Hadn't Dr. Emmanual insisted on him not looking back at all? 'Look to the future, my boy, there's a golden life ahead of you if you play your cards right . . . 'At least she liked music, and of the right kind. She would tolerate all his practising and realise his longing for peace and quiet. He hoped the other guests would not make too much fuss or expect him to waste valuable time answering questions. It was lucky the doctor had put him in with a friend of his: At least they would not lose contact and the doctor would probably come round to the house quite often in the day time.

I really must try and please her, his thoughts ran on. I've had more than enough of being pushed around and I'm due for a break. Only hope she likes me, though. It's so hard to please people. But I don't relish having to help in the guest house. The doctor did say something about that, instead of having to pay her. Imagine me with a sink full of dirty dishes, or having to carry a tray of expensive china. But I certainly have to be particular about my hands and she'd better know that . . .

13

Dr. Peter Emmanual was calling Giovanni now. He followed the professor down the steps beside the stage and into the main hall where a smiling Mrs. Williams was waiting. He must be on his best behaviour. Right, here goes . . .

'This is Giovanni, Liz.' Looking very pleased with himself, the doctor beamed at them both. 'Take him home, my dear, and look after him. He's yours for the season.'

Giovanni forced a smile as he put out his hand.

'Hallo, Mrs. Williams,' he ventured as brightly as possible. 'So pleased to meet you.'

After that he had little talking to do. The doctor was telling her all about him, thank goodness. She would know just where he had come from and something about his past life. You're *not* looking back, he told himself. You're going on from here to greater things and it's up to you to make the very best of this opportunity.

Elizabeth eyed the boy. How thin and neglected he looked, as if a good steak dinner was indicated! She would soon get rid of that pallor of his. Then, noting the faraway expression in those large black eyes, she wondered, Have I been too impetuous? Can I cope with a musician as well as my other guests? They won't mix. But this boy must have privacy for his practice: the visitors won't put up with that. I'll put him in Roger's room for the time being, and later on I can clear the attic and make a studio for him, far away from everybody . . .

Peter was speaking again:

'It is very good of my friend Mrs. Williams to agree to have you in her house, Gio. Off you go with her, and remember what I've told you.'

With that the doctor was gone.

That thin mac's no good for a night like this. There'll be April showers and cold winds. He'll need a thick warm coat to keep out the weather . . . Her mind ticking over, Elizabeth pulled open the door which led on to the pier. The full force of a sea wind met them. Giovanni seemed to be looking down at his feet as he pushed his way through the open door. In one hand he held the handle of a shabby green suitcase, in the other his black violin case. She decided to get him some pullovers tomorrow, and as for tonight she would find an extra blanket for him and move that electric fire into his room.

14

'D'you think you will like it here?' She was unsure quite how to break the ice, but anything, she felt, was better than silence.

'Not sure yet,' came the hesitant reply. 'I'll see how I get on. It is bound to be strange at first.' He sounded sad, tired and slightly overawed.

Their footsteps echoed clunk clunk on the wooden slats of the pier. A noisy sea-gull almost drowned conversation and the crunching of shingle receding on the beach was making resounding noises down below. Further on the huge waves were hitting the over hanging rocks of the Great Orme on the headland, thundering and crashing like the loud music in the middle of a symphony. Whatever she tried to say would be inaudible. Elizabeth knew. They walked on in silence.

Elizabeth was almost asleep.

Could she be dreaming? No, it was real enough. The bedside clock registered almost one-thirty and yet musical sounds were coming from the next bedroom. Clearly, in the familiar golden tones, she recognised the scale of G Major in three octaves, then a succession of minor chords and a snatch from a symphony. The violin sounded unusually loud, breaking the silence of the night to penetrate the whole house.

Whatever had she let herself in for in agreeing to accommodate a particularly keen virtuoso violinist? Surely she owed something to her paying guests, now doing their utmost to get a good night's sleep?

Turning over languidly, she pulled the blankets well over her head. If the visitors disliked the sound of music, then it was they who would have to go.

Chapter 2

'Swallow Tree Gardens' was a solidly built Victorian residence containing eight bedrooms on three floors. A narrow staircase led up to a spacious attic ideal for storing cots, bed linen and spare furniture. The house, in Roger's family for many years, had passed down in his name, his parents having made sufficient capital out of it to be able to retire in their early fifties to a small bungalow near Caernarvon.

The house stood in its own grounds. A front wall had been removed to make space for six or eight cars, and behind this area was a thriving shrubbery requiring very little attention. Early rhododendrons were already coming into bloom in glorious shades of mauve, pink and red, and two stately magnolias flanked either side of the glass porch, their cream flowers standing up like huge candles.

All rooms had fine views, the front ones of the sea, the others of the rolling hills which stretched out as far as the Conwy Valley and far away towards Snowdonia. Cattle and sheep grazed contentedly on the luscious green grass and each field was bordered by huge woodland trees, oak, silver birch and sycamore, their leaves now thick and in varying shades of green.

Not over house-proud, but clean and tidy for all that, Elizabeth kept the house in good order, making full use of labour-saving devices. The dining room overlooked the garden where two huge lawns were surrounded by sturdy rose bushes and a mass of sweet smelling lilac. Within a few weeks golden laburnum would add a rich colour to the scene.

At the other end of the house was a square, oak-panelled lounge, fitted with a carpet with an overall pattern reminiscent of falling leaves in Autumn. Three coffee tables and a dozen television chairs in red, brown and green were scattered about the room, and visitors had access to a large bookcase, generously filled with paper-backs, magazines and games of Scrabble and Monopoly. Rooms were heated by means of old-fashioned electric fires, central heating being the next item on Elizabeth's list of improvements.

An annexe had been added to the rear of the house, far enough away to be private, and out of reach of the noise of traffic and children. Here Elizabeth had her music room and private lounge, where her musical guests were entertained. During the season, the entire Palm Court Orchestra was invited to lunch, followed by an afternoon of music around her grand piano.

The financial arrangement was that Roger covered rates and electric bills, whilst takings from the guests paid for a gardener, a cleaning woman, and the maintenance and renovation of the premises.

Ever quick and alert, Elizabeth never wasted a minute but made every effort to get through her daily chores so as to get back to her piano, her records and her concerts. No time for make-up or elaborate hair-dos, she combined efficiency with speed, and her look of determination gave her a quiet confidence and an air of self-assurance.

In her opinion, all fashion was over-rated and the latest styles a waste of valuable money. She looked good in smart clothes when the occasion demanded it, but felt more at home in casuals. She would work her way around the golf course in double quick time, or climb a mountain while others were still studying the map, but all this was done in the interests of keeping fit, so determined was she never to succumb to the numerous ailments which formed an absorbing topic of conversation for the masses.

Elizabeth made copious lists headed 'letters to be written', 'people to visit' and 'jobs to be done', keeping them in prominent places and rarely forgetting anything. At all times she preferred her own company and never sought out people for companionship. Given the right person, she thoroughly enjoyed an intellectual conversation but would rather walk five miles alone than be lumbered with an empty-headed chatterbox. The only time she indulged in small-talk was where politeness demanded it, or when she felt thoroughly sorry for some lonely or bed-ridden soul. At such times she radiated energy, rushing in like a breath of fresh air, and the very enthusiasm in her voice served as a tonic, a stimulant or a sedative, whatever was required.

17

Elizabeth took care not to neglect her parents at Warrington and was in the habit of visiting them three times a year, taking birthday presents and Christmas goodies. She regularly invited them for a week to her home during the summer, treating them to the various shows which she knew they would enjoy.

Everything was bought in bulk; she hated trudging round the big stores and never indulged in window gazing. With an hour on her hands in the city, she would make for the nearest library or art gallery and thoroughly enjoy her own company among the artistic and literary treasures.

Elizabeth would bend over backwards to give away, without thought of repayment, what she really needed for herself. Impulsive and rash, she would have signed away a whole fortune, on the spur of the moment, if her compassionate instincts were thereby satisfied. She could be as gentle as a lamb when necessary, soft as putty if the right person came along to influence her in the right way. Like a broody hen clucking over her young chicks, so Elizabeth would protect and nourish anyone under-privileged, indulge in their whims, and thoroughly take them under her wing. Under that dominating nature cried out something soft and affectionate, a tiny voice craving love and admiration. When off duty she loved nothing better than the thrill of soft breezes blowing through her hair, the scent of wild flowers in the woods and the twitter of birds in the trees. Such simple pleasures were to her like ambrosia and nectar, and she often declared that not for all the money in the world would she have changed places with any city dweller, business commuter, or office drudge.

Each summer season, Elizabeth chose her au-pair girl with special care, and this summer she had been particularly lucky. Life was obviously fascinating for young Gretta, whose big blue eyes continually sparkled with excitement. Small, slender and elfin faced, she wore her smooth dark hair hanging about her shoulders, as sleek and shiny as polished ebony.

Gretta's shorts and tee shirts which she wore off-duty showed off her shapely legs to perfection, but Elizabeth insisted upon a clean white apron over a check gingham dress for the hours between five and eight, when dinner was being served.

She met Giovanni with a mixture of surprise and disappointment.

'I find 'im 'ansome,' she giggled, after an unsuccessful attempt to flirt with him in her flippant way. 'But he is not as I am,

18

looking for fun. Glum and serious he is, and not one word to say. See 'im in a disco and 'e be lost. 'Schuchtern' he is, or shy as you say in English. But I wake 'im up. I make 'im live. 'E be different soon, you see.'

Fortunately Giovanni was not there to hear this analysis. Elizabeth was quick to reprimand Gretta, in the best German she could produce, for criticising a guest under her roof.

Early in the morning, sparkle and fun shone out of the girl's radiant face as she danced around the dining room in a twirl of excitement, singing at the top of her soprano voice. In no time at all she would master English — and probably get a smattering of Welsh too. She was already half way there, and anyway, it was fun to be in a foreign country for a whole summer and meet all types. This guest house was a real challenge and as for young Gio — she'd soon fix *him*!

Elizabeth floated on a cloud of ecstasy for a whole week. Completely at peace with the world, she felt at least she could have forgiven Roger for all the heart-ache she had suffered. I must write to him, she resolved, send an affectionate letter and include some of his favourite after-shave, the kind he cannot buy out there. There was a comfortable feeling inside her and a distinct sense of exultation as she went about starry-eyed, even inwardly reprimanding herself for having been so harsh and unforgiving. Roger was basically a good kind chap, and no amount of estrangement could ever bring Timothy back, so why prolong the agony?

Roger usually came home for the three hottest months of the year and so he was due about the middle of June. He would spend his time on fishing and shooting expeditions. Elizabeth always fed him well and their conversation remained pleasant and relaxed, even if lacking in affection.

What would Roger think about this violin player in his house? Would he ever understand? He had always declared her to be obsessed with 'all this classical stuff', as he called it. He preferred a brass band, or a small group with a lot of beat to it. Anyway, his possible reaction didn't really matter at the moment and things had a habit of sorting themselves out if one didn't worry too much. By the time Roger came home, she would have made all sorts of alterations to her schedule.

Elizabeth was well aware of the arrangement for Giovanni to help in the guest house in lieu of board and lodgings. As the second week went by, she was forced to conclude that nobody could expect a boy of his temperament to lower his mind to kitchen work. Anyway, she reminded herself, he'd insisted on taking on the vegetable peeling and spent many an hour on the patio with bucket and saucepan and one of those safe potato peelers. Slow, yes — but the job got done even if, as he always admitted, his mind was far away during the whole process.

He was most unpredictable, she observed, sometimes getting up at six to make for the beach or the hills; at other times he'd be sound asleep, unconscious of the breakfast gong, and have to be prodded and shaken in order to be in time for the morning concert at eleven.

'It's hard to keep normal hours, Elizabeth,' he would say as he dashed downstairs and swallowed half a cup of tea. 'Some nights my brain works on long past midnight and sleep does not come till three. And so I'm just like a log in the mornings. Thanks a lot for calling me in time.'

His repair jobs were a disaster. Whatever he tackled, something inevitably went wrong. The screw-head would come off, the nail would split the wood or the glass would shatter. Too cautious to risk an injury to his fingers, he would fumble around until Elizabeth arrived on the scene and, kindly but firmly, ordered him off. 'Not to worry, the job can easily wait,' she would assure him. 'I'll get a man in tomorrow . . .'

Why did he always keep out of Gretta's way? Could it be becasue she was too noisy or too frivolous for him? A pity he hadn't more sense of humour. It was the one thing that spoilt him. But how he loved to invade her kitchen, his violin under his chin as he practised some new piece. There he would stand in the middle of her kitchen area, awaiting her approval, her suggestions, her encouragement.

Why wasn't he more interested in food, she contemplated? Never particularly hungry, he had to be coaxed like a child, and in the end it was always the plainest of dishes he preferred. Give him a plate of spaghetti or macaroni and he'd polish it off with relish — but that, of course, must be his Italian background.

Giovanni confided in her about his unhappy childhood, and how he was beaten by his father.

'He thought of me as an infant prodigy, you see, to be moulded in his hands. D'you know, he actually broke three violin bows over my head? He lashed out if he heard me make so much as one mistake.'

20

Elizabeth winced, visualizing such punishment meted out to an innocent child.

'I wonder it didn't put you off music altogether.' Her tone was one of surprise, to think he had stuck it out so well.

The boy stared ahead of him, reliving the past, his voice bitter and accusing:

'Some people can play an instrument and haven't a clue how to teach. My father expected too much from a child. I remember many a time, wet eyed and running nose, doing my utmost to get my small fingers in the right place on the strings, with my fiddle covered in tears. Sometimes I think he must have been mad.'

'But surely your mother . . .' Elizabeth broke off, her face showing nothing but shock.

'She did nothing,' he shrugged his shoulders. 'Either she was too scared to interfere or she was a weak sort of woman. I hardly remember her: I was taken into care at the age of eight. The neighbours had reported the way I was being treated, and the teachers confirmed the bruises which continually appeared on my limbs.'

Giovanni knew that his father was born in Rome and there was a history of musical talent in the family, his grandmother being the famous operatic mezzosoprano, Francesa da Rico, his grandfather a conductor at La Scala, Milan.

His father, Frederico Malvolio, had come to England between the wars to try and find work, and had played in several London cinemas for the silent movies, later moving to Manchester, where he had met Giovanni's mother. Heavy drinker that he was, he had in his sober moments nourished great ambitions for his only son. But he had expected the impossible: a child, even at the tender age of seven, attempting difficult passages from memory. His hot Italian temperament leaving him devoid of patience, he frequently flew into a rage and threw things about if he heard a single note out of tune, as he stood over Giovanni in the hot parlour on a Sunday afternoon, with the blinds drawn, while the happy shrieks of children enjoying themselves could be heard from the area down below.

Such desolate early experiences had given Giovanni a distorted view on life. He found it difficult to trust people, was frightened to show affection, and had become generally unsettled and un-cooperative. He had no regrets when he was taken away from his parents; on the contrary it was a relief in many ways. But he was thankful that he had inherited his mother's gentle outlook rather than his father's turbulent nature.

Giovanni had hated the lack of privacy at the children's home. He had loathed having to share a room, wear handed down clothing, conform to strict house rules, observe strict time tables and clear away all his things into a locker just because the bell had rung for supper.

Somewhere inside him was a deep sense of reverence. He loved to go out and stare into the sky, observing the stars and contemplating his future. He would pray earnestly for something to brighten up his life and give it more shape. His entry into Swallow Tree Gardens appeared to be a partial answer to this prayer and had certainly given him an insight into the kind of life he really wanted to live.

He had a habit of spreading out his hands and examining them carefully to ensure they were unblemished. He avoided the jagged edges of tins and jars, or manual jobs which might affect the free use of his arm, wrist and fingers for delicate violin playing.

His unhappy childhood had put him completely off the idea of love and marriage. In any case, he argued, what time would he have for a wife and children with all these hours of solid practising? And was he not already married to his violin?

Giovanni hated discord or argument of any kind. He had determined quite early on that he would not be dragged into the army if a war should break out: no, he would refuse point blank, even if it meant going to prison. He had read so much of the New Testament that he was positive it was wrong to fight or kill. He was a student of the Scriptures, and where ever he went his Bible went with him as well as his violin.

He hated the idea of being disliked by anyone. He felt inadequate and inferior in many ways, but if only people would like him for what he was he would be content. He tried so hard to please them. He insisted the world would be a better place if only people were more peace-loving — if they would get on with their own lives without all this quarrelling and crime.

Timid and unobtrusive, Giovanni would seek the sanctuary of a corner with his books and papers, and there he would spend many a happy hour studying, reading and contemplating. He was an out and out genius — but a dreamer. For all the lack of culture in his background, he had emerged a skilled, proficient soloist with a fantastic memory and an aptitude for composing well beyond his years. But his only asset was his musical know-how. Ask him to change a wheel or mend a fuse and he would look as helpless as a baby. But how he handled his violin! One day he would set the world on fire with that expertise — that gift of interpretation which left audiences spell-bound.

Like many deprived people Giovanni Malvolio had a chip on his shoulder. The world, he felt, owed him something for those years when he had missed out, when he had been roughly treated, pushed around from foster-parent to foster-parent, each one complaining of his lack of co-operation and general aloofness.

Ignored in the playground as a 'softie' he had been when he had refused all rough games; but how could he have exposed his body to the tremors of football when any slight injury could have interrupted his fiddle playing? Anything, in fact, which stood in the way of his daily two hour practice was to him the end of the world.

He would have liked to have exchanged his scraggy figure for that of an Olympic trainer but would have begrudged the training time. His one-track mind had excluded exercise and left him in a permanent groove. Like at college, when he had just snatched at his food, craving to return to his study, his manuscript and his violin.

Elizabeth and Giovanni spent many an hour in the music room where the boy would confide in her. It was cosy having someone there to share her love of music, and Elizabeth knew a fulfilment, on an intellectual plane, such as she had not experienced before.

'Did you ever see your parents again?' she asked as Giovanni sprawled in one of her deep armchairs and she sat on the leather couch opposite.

'They did visit me at the home, and I was even allowed to go back with them for a weekend . . . But it didn't work out. Later on I was put out to more foster-parents and, to make matters worse, never fitted in anywhere. Everybody said how unsociable I was!'

Thoroughly relaxed, Giovanni lowered his body further and deeper into the easy chair, his feet spread out across the carpet. It was easy to enjoy the joke now that it was all over, but **Elizabeth felt nothing but pity for him :**

'What a traumatic experience for one so young.'

'Actually, I think the rough and tumble of life helped me to mature early,' he replied, studying the pattern on the carpet. 'Sometimes I feel I was never a child at all. I had no interest in sport, pop music was a deafening hullaballoo, television a waste of precious time.'

'Did you never have a girl friend?'

'Never!' came the decisive reply. 'I always found it impossible to communicate with girls. I suppose I haven't got what it takes. My head is usually in a book. And at that time I was also working hard on my composing — great fun. The School Magazine made good use of my songs and I won a number of prizes — but it was for the joy of it that I carried on. I got such a kick out of melody and harmony and had to express myself.'

When talking of his achievements, Giovanni's tone became animated. His only friend, he explained, happened to be his violin teacher, who often invited him to his home to show off his playing to his friends. It was between the ages of twelve and sixteen, he went on, that he had gained his technique. Spotted as the most promising pupil at the school, he had received special coaching for the County Youth Orchestra. From then he had progressed to being their youngest leader at fourteen.

The scholarship to the College of Music at Manchester had been the turning point, the period in which Giovanni had devoted his whole life to improving his technique. Dr. Peter Emmanual had attended the Students' Concert where he had rendered the Tchaikovsky Violin Concerto. And, there and then, the doctor had decided to take over his career.

By the end of the third week, Elizabeth noted that the boy had softened up even more, confiding to her some of his most intimate thoughts. He looked altogether happier and, she judged, was getting more enjoyment out of life.

Most evenings, after the concert, they would make their way to the music room or to her private lounge for relaxation. By that time Gretta would have finished her clearing away and be content to join the visitors in the public lounge, or take her transistor radio to her room. Occasionally there would be a disco in the area, and she would accompany another au-pair girl for an hour or two, but the rule was that she must be back by twelve.

Elizabeth and Giovanni discussed the enjoyable concert wherein Les had accompanied the cellist in the slow movement of the

Dvorak Concerto. Particularly cordial during the interval, Peter Emmanual had promised to call at Swallow Tree Gardens for a chat and an exchange of views. It had been a perfect evening in every way, and now the clock on Elizabeth's mantelpiece struck eleven as Giovanni thumbed through her collection of records in the cabinet, sitting cross legged and leaning against the wall paper. She entered, coffee pot in hand, and placed a tray of assorted savouries on a nearby table.

'What a perfect home you have, Elizabeth, for a music lover,' he remarked as she handed him a cup of coffee with a huge blob of cream floating on its surface. 'Do you know you have well over five hundred records here, besides all those cassettes? What you haven't got can't be worth having!'

Elizabeth smiled at the compliment. It gave her a warm feeling inside, as if she were needed and the turn in the boy's life hinged entirely on her.

She had brought her attempts at composing to the lounge and now, somewhat diffidently, presented them for Giovanni's comments. After studying each song thoughtfully between sips of coffee and mouthfuls of pork-pie, he laid the pile of manuscripts on the record cabinet and then sat quite still.

'Don't keep me waiting for your verdict, Gio!' Elizabeth blurted, unable to bear his silence a moment longer. 'Should they go in the bin, or is there any hope?'

His face lit up encouragingly as he picked up the top manuscript and turned the pages.

'If I were your tutor, Elizabeth, I would say they are a good attempt for a beginner and show undoubted promise. However, this chord here is not really in harmony with that one underneath it, and that short song doesn't end with a perfect cadence.'

His tone was kind and a definite smile lurked at the corners of his mouth as she interrupted:

'That's all very well! Seeing you are *not* my tutor, what does the famous maestro have to say?'

'I tell you with confidence that I myself could bring these songs up to publication standard — and, if you approve, it will be my pleasure.'

In her relief Elizabeth burst out laughing, and Giovanni joined in. It was an enormous boost to her morale to know that, after all, there was hope for that dusty pile of songs over which she had laboured some years ago, and she might yet see her name in print.

'Eat up these vol-au-vents, Gio,' she commanded. 'You're far too thin for any guest of mine. I must make it my job to put some flesh on those bones and some colour into those cheeks.'

With the savouries out of the way, Giovanni became suddenly serious as he joined her on the couch and stuffed a cushion behind his back.

'There is something I wish to tell you, Elizabeth . . . my most sacred secret. I have three important ambitions in life, about each of which I have thought a great deal. May I enlighten you?'

'Of course,' she murmured, hanging on every word, and he sat upright, arms folded, body leaning slightly forward.

'First, more than anything else, I would like to own one of those rare Italian violins. A tutor of mine had a Guarnarius and he lent it to me once for solos. Elizabeth, it was out of this world! I shall never forget just how that instrument responded or how thrilling it was to handle.'

His tone had become whimsical, as if the whole idea was completely out of his grasp. Then he took a deep breath, his eyes shining with contemplation.

'My second ambition is to play the whole Elgar Concerto from memory before an audience at the Royal Festival Hall.'

Giovanni's features might suggest he was living in a world of fantasy, but he spoke with earnestness and conviction and Elizabeth felt pride that a man so young could have such high aspirations.

'I've always considered the Elgar to be the most difficult of the lot,' she replied. 'Have you tackled it?'

'Not yet, I'm still on the easier ones. It will come later though.'

There was a pause until Elizabeth ventured: 'And your third ambition?' How exciting it was, she thought.

'My third, Elizabeth, is the greatest one of all — to write a symphony in four movements, and to be there, in the front row, when it is performed in a London concert hall.'

'A symphony!' Elizabeth exclaimed: 'A whole symphony . . . the high ideal, the ultimate! The ambition of every composer. Oh, Giovanni, how I do admire your pluck! Carry on like this and you will certainly be famous. I only hope I live to see it. And now, having got that off your chest, shall we hear one of those symphonies on which to model your own? We have time for one of the shorter ones before we call it a day.'

She crossed to the cabinet and looked through the titles.

26

'What about Mozart's thirty-ninth?'

A feeling of serenity filled the whole room. Twenty minutes of perfect bliss ensued as they listened to every note.

Suddenly Elizabeth jerked upward, startled by the sound of a door banging and then heavy footsteps in her kitchen area. It was almost midnight and the rest of the house was silent. The last movement of the symphony was reaching its climax, a sleepy Giovanni resting his head against a cushion. The room was in semi-darkness.

All at once, as if a hurricane had burst upon them, the peaceful scene was invaded as a man rushed in to switch off the music centre. Then he turned, his lips curled in a contemptuous sneer, and Elizabeth faltered: 'Roger . . .' He had been drinking, she could see.

'This is my house,' he grated, 'and that is my bedroom. Is it this fella's stuff in there? If so he'd better clear it out quick.'

Too stunned to reply, she shook all over. Her throat was dry, her knees were weak, her heart pounded against her ribs.

'Your job, my lady,' he went on, 'is looking after visitors, not spending all your time and money on that high faluting music of yours! If you go on like this much longer, you'll have no visitors left. You're just crazy about music.'

All the blood had drained from Elizabeth's face. She tried to speak, but still nothing came.

'I get home at nine o'clock to find my wife gone off to a concert. I decide to go out for a drink, but first I go to my room — and what do I find? Another man's things. Get out, d'you hear? Clear off!'

Roger waved a fist at Giovanni, who stared helplessly from him to Elizabeth. Her mind raced. For his sake she must keep calm. Hadn't he suffered enough in his short life without being thrown out again?

She blamed herself for using Roger's room. But how could she have known he would arrive like this out of the blue — and why did he have to get himself so dreadfully drunk?

She knew she must choose her words with the utmost care. Most important of all, no harm must come to Giovanni. There was no time to waste, and very little time in which to think, as she got to her feet and stood facing her husband.

Chapter 3

At first Elizabeth felt nothing but fury, her mind brimming over with indignation. Then, suddenly, like the calm of a troubled sea after a storm, her resentment disappeared. This man who confronted her, much the worse for drink, wasn't the real Roger and should be dealt with accordingly.

Persuading Giovanni to remain where he was, she took Roger's arm and placed her other arm on his shoulder. Smiling into his face like a mother dealing with a difficult child, she led him towards his room.

'Cool down, Roger,' she said soothingly. 'You've had a difficult day and a long flight. By far the best place for you is bed. Don't you agree? You'll feel so much better in the morning . . .'

He struggled feebly in her grasp, obviously at the end of his tether.

'It's my room that young guy's got, and this is my house . . . What's he doing here anyway? . . . What's going on?'

His voice slurred, he could hardly keep on his feet.

'Quite right,' Elizabeth replied calmly. 'I intend clearing the attic for him. If only you'd let me know you were coming I could have been ready with a hot meal for you. As for what's going on — nothing. He's just a boy in need of a home, a mere boy. So don't for heaven's sake make anything out of this, Roger! I'm not like that, as you know quite well — I get all my emotional satisfaction out of music and have no need of any other. Now do you understand?'

It worked. In a matter of minutes she had grabbed all Giovanni's belongings, got Roger into bed, and Giovanni to the settee for the night.

'We'll clear the attic tomorrow,' she promised him. 'It will

28

make an ideal studio, and so long as you confine your practice to the afternoons, when the visitors are out, it should work.'

Her relief was indescribable: it was as if she had shed two huge sacks of potatoes from her shoulders after struggling with them up a winding staircase for a very long time.

Roger came down to breakfast in a better frame of mind. Within hours he would be catching his plane, his only reason for appearing so suddenly being, as he explained, that he had been sent to collect some plans and specifications for an installation at a hospital in Jedda. Head Office being at Wrexham, and he having to travel so near to home, he had decided to pay Elizabeth a surprise call.

Over a hearty breakfast, and without a single reference to the previous night, he remarked somewhat disinterestedly:

'Bit of a rumpus at the Council meeting, luv, so I heard in the boozer last night. Seems they almost came to blows.'

Refilling the toast rack, Elizabeth buttered a slice for herself as she replied absently:

'Nothing unusual, quite a few pig-headed ones on the council now. Not a bit like it used to be.'

'There's a split over the lease of the Pier this summer. Seems it went through on a majority vote of one. Half of them are strongly opposed to things as they are and want a disco, slot machines and a fun-fair. The town is behind the times, they reckon, and we'd be better off financially.'

As Roger talked an uncomfortable feeling of compassion swept through Elizabeth. Before many hours, this husband, now enjoying his egg and bacon under their roof, would be thousands of miles away. Guilt struck like an arrow within her heart, painfully bringing home to her the irony of last night's argument. There should have been no question of 'his room' or 'her room'. Here was the man with whom she had shared many happy years. Weak minded he may have been, careless and negligent — but he was still her husband.

She noticed how aged he looked as a result of the climate out there. He had a distinct bald patch these days and his short brown hair was greying at the temples. There were lines across his forehead which she had not noticed before, and the hot sun had weathered the skin of a once handsome face to give him the appearance of a man the wrong side of forty. Within an

29

hour, he was gone with a peck kiss on her cheek and a cheery 'See you in June' before the taxi swept him away.

Roger's remarks about the council meeting were nothing new. There had always been an element of doubt as to whether Dr. Emmanual would get the lease for the pier head pavilion for his concerts. True, by the skin of his teeth, the concerts were on for this season, but already an unpleasant under-current had started its course in the town.

With Naomi's help, Elizabeth had formed the 'Friends of the Orchestra Association' to combat this opposition: a keen group of music lovers whose aim was to help forward the smooth running of the concerts both for the musicians and their audience. Such was the recent increase in their numbers that the last meeting at the Dutch Cafe had been attended by sixty or more.

Elizabeth remembered the chairman's remarks as they had all sipped their coffee in the pleasant cafe atmosphere four days ago:

'Ladies and gentlemen, after two weeks of pier head concerts, I am sure we can all agree that we have made an excellent start. The sixteen members of the Palm Court Orchestra have already displayed their talent and, in particular, we must single out for praise Dr. Emmanual's discovery, little Giovanni, whose exquisite playing has thrilled us all. We look forward with keen anticipation to more items from this youngster's repertoire. With more campaigning in the town, and more advertising, to say nothing of another bring-and-buy sale to increase our funds, I am confident we will make our concerts more popular and attract bigger audiences for the rest of the season.'

Mention had been made of the excellent flute solos which had almost raised the roof one evening. Elizabeth had announced her intention of inviting the orchestra to 'Swallow Tree Gardens' for lunch on May 25th: she would need ten helpers as hosts for the occasion. Much enthusiasm had been shown, volunteers being far in excess of requirements. With only three weeks to go, the arrangements would soon have to be finalised.

It was decided to insert articles in the 'Weekly Chronicle' praising the good tone of the town with its high class of visitor, a point worth mentioning when it was compared with other resorts where the promenade had become one long stream of chippies, bingo halls and pubs.

'We may be Victorian in some of our ways and tastes,' one

speaker had continued, 'but this fine holiday town is proud of its heritage. We prefer to be Victorian and Classical than to be labelled a modern pop-music society, with all its discordant screechings and reverberating clatter.'

Elizabeth recalled her conversation with Naomi on the way home.

'Last season was a real struggle to keep the concerts going right through,' Elizabeth had remarked in anxious tones.

'But you managed it.'

'Yes, by means of a united effort. The opposition on the council was terrific. They worked hard to boycott our concerts. They even instructed the pier staff to delay the times of opening up the pavilion, and so there we were, queueing up in the wet and cold and wind of many an evening last summer, till just before starting time.'

'That would have put some people off for sure.' Naomi sounded concerned.

'All the regular hard-liners continued to attend. I remember, too, how they got the cafe staff to close just before the interval in the evenings and so prevent the audience from having their coffee.'

'How beastly. A rotten trick!'

'The same with the morning concerts on Tuesdays and Thursdays. The staff who run the kiosks for newspapers, cigarettes and chocolates deliberately delayed their opening so the audience could not pop in for what they wanted before the concert.'

'I can see what we're up against, Liz. Could be quite a problem.'

'Worse still, my dear, I shall never forget one evening late in April when we shivered for the whole two hours. My feet were like ice. I still don't know how the musicians played in tune.'

'So they persuaded someone not to put on the heat?'

'Yes, even that. Another thing, they tried hard to get a concert going in the other pavilion in opposition to ours — TV stars, big placards and lights all over the town. The admission charge was about half our own. They want Dr. Emmanual to be a flop and our audience to decrease until we finally have to give up.'

'You know something, Liz?' Her eyes sparkling with enthusiasm, Naomi had grabbed Elizabeth's arm. 'The average age of our audiences is well past forty. What we need in this town is a

College of Music, or at least a Music Section at our Tech. That could draw all the young people to our concerts and infuse some young blood into the whole set-up.'

A college of music, Elizabeth had mused next day. What a splendid idea. She would certainly mention it to Peter at the next opportunity.

'I've served all the breakfasts and it's after ten, Mrs. Williams, but is Gio there? Oh no. Not anywhere.'

Gretta's English, initially poor, was improving daily. This morning she looked anxious as she entered the kitchen with a tray of crockery and made her way to the sink.

'He must be in his room,' Elizabeth replied as she loaded the dishwasher with plates of various sizes. 'Still asleep, I'll wager.'

'No — he is not there!' Gretta sounded alarmed. 'I go up to see, and what do I find? Bed all tidy and smooth — he not sleep there for sure — his concert suit over a chair thrown — his swim suit not there — his track suit also gone!'

Elizabeth looked up then, her face full of concern. Amazing how perceptive the German girl was. Having raced up three flights of stairs to the attic, she had already weighed up the situation and even knew which clothes were missing from Giovanni's room.

'He wouldn't want to swim so early in the year. The sea must be very cold and quite rough too.' As she spoke, Elizabeth shivered.

'And he not a swimmer strong like I. A race we had in the pool last week. Five metres I was in front of him. He puffing and blowing and me still strong and ready again to swim.'

Gretta's words only added to the anxiety of the occasion.

'Last night, in the lounge, one of the visitors tell me he see man on beach at about eleven o'clock — young and dark-haired, with black and white track suit.'

Gretta was obviously pleased to be able to offer so much information, although her face looked troubled and her voice was subdued.

Elizabeth's mind flashed back. Yes, Giovanni had gone straight to his room after the concert. Hadn't he mentioned a headache? For once he had not made his usual appearance in her lounge. Where ever could he be? A cold April night, the sea roaring and throwing up huge white waves before crashing noisily on to the rocks. It was most unusual.

The boy was unpredictable, she admitted. Sometimes he ate ravenously; at other times he ate nothing. He did take long walks over the mountains, but always in the day time. He had confided that he was best able to compose when alone, far away from civilisation — in the fresh air and high winds of a Welsh mountain. Inspiration in such surroundings came to him like a gift from above. But it would be ridiculous if he were out walking now. Why, he had been missing for almost twelve hours! Mingled with her anxiety and near despair, Elizabeth was vexed by his thoughtlessness.

What an unusual person he really was. Fidgety and unsettled, she mused, he would move from room to room, uncertain what to do next. Often, during conversations, his eyes would become vacant and pre-occupied, as if his thoughts were elsewhere. Whilst making a pretence of listening he would in reality be miles away.

Then Elizabeth had a mental picture of the beach and that treacherous path which led high up amongst the cliffs. They were known to be dangerous; many a boy had lost his life there attempting to retrieve sea-gulls' eggs. Please God, she prayed, don't have me called out again to identify a floating body in the sea, Please make it safe for Giovanni . . .

The next two hours seemed like an eternity, her thoughts tossing about like so much coloured washing in a tumble-drier. Finally, in sheer desperation, she telephoned Peter in case Giovanni had gone there or the doctor had heard some conversation which might indicate the boy's whereabouts.

'I've no idea what to think, Liz,' Peter sighed. 'He's most unconventional and, at times, quite perplexing. Do let me know as soon as you get any news: I shall not rest till I know. He could have broken his arm and no fiddle player should take risks, especially one who plays solos.'

That's true, Elizabeth pondered, an arm or a leg or even worse. But all Peter thought about was how it would affect his concerts, while what worried her was just where Gio was — and if he were safe!

Chapter 4

Elizabeth knew in her heart that she was overreacting, but the knowledge made it no easier. With all her efficiency and business know-how, she was after all only a woman, and a mother too. All afternoon she occupied herself as usual with preparing the evening meal, mechanically filling large saucepans with peeled potatoes, carrots and cauliflower. As nicely browned apple tarts came out of the oven, smelling deliciously of cloves and cinnamon, so Welsh leg of lamb took their place and started sizzling appetisingly. The asparagus soup could wait, also the custard, and soon, she knew, Gretta would be laying the tables. Yet the whole house seemed dead without the golden strains of the violin which usually came floating down about this time.

At five o'clock, seated on the piano stool, she placed her hands on the white keys but felt nothing. She skimmed through a Nocturne by her beloved Chopin, but her eyes saw nothing. Why did she feel so lost? Was it the boy or the music?

Even in childhood Elizabeth had been stirred and even excited by the sound of music. She well remembered, at the age of five, causing a ripple of laughter amongst her mother's friends at a church concert, when she had clapped eagerly and shouted, 'I like that pretty noise. It's beautiful.' At six she had taken her first piano lessons, and within eight months a proud teacher had suggested that she take her exam, which she had passed with merit.

During the years that followed she had progressed from scales to sonatas and then to concertos, practising for hours without having to be coaxed or bribed. The German grand piano was her eighteenth birthday present from her parents, and the day of that gift stood out in her memory as one of her proudest.

34

She recalled on one occasion attending a symphony concert alone, at Liverpool Philharmonic Hall. So exhilarated had she been, so carried away by the revelation of hearing Sibelius' second symphony for the first time, that she had no recollection whatever of the journey home. Her ecstasy had known no bounds as she tried to explain to her bewildered parents that she must have made for the car park, manoeuvred her way across the city and travelled the seventy miles, without coming out of her trance. 'You know, Mum, there's a tune going on in my head all the time. Is it unusual, do you think?' She had done her utmost to explain but her parents remained puzzled.

She had met Roger at the local Tech. where both were taking their City and Guilds, he in the electrical engineering department, she in a course of catering. His lightheartedness and good humour had appealed to her. He could bring her out of a serious or sombre mood by means of laughter and they seemed to make a good pair. Always impulsive, she had agreed to a short engagement and later to an elaborate wedding, Roger looking ahead to the time when his parents would hand over the prosperous guest house to him, and confident that Elizabeth's knowledge of catering and her general efficiency and seriousness would be an asset to him. He was really the practical one. He was witty and a good mixer, whereas she was a bit unsociable, but it had not seemed to matter at that time, and never had it occurred to either of them that there could be such a thing as incompatibility. On the surface the marriage had been all right, with both sets of parents showing nothing but approval and giving every possible help. Elizabeth had felt rather like a prisoner at first when the guest house had begun to fill up and she was compelled to devote between ten and sixteen hours to mundane jobs on sultry summer days.

What a joy Timothy had been to them, she recalled. They had agreed it would be wise to get extra help in the house during those busy years. At that time the child and the housework had occupied first place in her life, with Roger coming second and music certainly taking a back seat. For years the piano had hardly ever been opened and there was no chance to hear her favourite records, Roger being keen on guitars and electric organs, but both agreeing that a good Welsh male voice choir was worth booking seats for.

It was only after the loss of their child that Elizabeth had

35

turned her heart and soul back into classical music. She had become involved in the summer concerts and with Dr. Peter Emmanual, experiencing a feeling of shame and guilt on more than one occasion as she compared his tastes and ideals with those of Roger. If only she could have met Peter when they were both young: how very different life would have been. As they conversed she would gaze into his eyes and catch there a sparkle of admiration which sent a warm glow through her whole body. Emotions such as these were quite sufficient to satisfy Elizabeth. If she did have a crush on Peter Emmanual, it was his gift of music which thrilled her more than anything else.

On the other hand Roger was the complete outdoor type, tall and strong with big green eyes set in a ruddy wind-swept face which seemed to have a charm all its own. His ready smile displayed pearly white teeth which appeared all the brighter against a healthy tan. Good tempered and easily pleased, he never made demands, giving in to Elizabeth's wishes for the sake of peace and quiet. Easy going and inoffensive, he resigned himself to whatever came his way, making the best of any obstacle and keeping his cool when under pressure. He enjoyed a night out with the boys and only very occasionally got drunk.

His shot gun and his fishing tackle were still Roger's best friends, treasured above all else. Tired but happy, he would arrive home with a couple of pheasant and a wild goose in his bag, slipping unobtrusively into the kitchen and closing the door. The plucking and dressing completed, he'd present his offering to Elizabeth on a clean plate. She would show her delight at the time but, quite illogically, pass critical remarks at other times about the cruelty of mutilating such lovely birds and the inhumanity of blood sports. Such inconsistencies left Roger speechless.

He had never fully understood the dreadful fuss she had made over the death of Tim. Such things did happen, after all, with nobody really to blame. Why could she too not take it in her stride? Instead she had pushed him out of her life like a stray dog in the cold air on a winter's night.

For Roger life had not ended there. Life was still full of pleasures, man's pleasures. Life in Saudi Arabia was a challenge, an adventure, with a thrill all its own, and so he never complained.

Elizabeth was jerked back to reality as an excited Gretta rushed into the room with waving arms.

'Gio is back! Been out walking he has, silly twit! I say before he is crazy — and I am right.'

Astonished, Elizabeth stood up as Gretta continued.

'In the kitchen he is, washing his hands. Such a mess I never saw. Just covered in dust!'

Elizabeth hurried out of the room towards the kitchen. She could hear Giovanni's voice, and it had the warmth and glow of bright sunshine on a bed of Spring flowers.

'Where on earth have you been?' she said sternly, as though to a child. 'And what a state you're in!'

'Oh, Elizabeth, it's good to be back. Do you know, I must have walked twenty miles.'

As he rinsed his hands under the cold tap, she eyed his dishevelled hair, his soiled clothing and muddy shoes.

'Where have you been all this time, Gio? We've worried ourselves to death about you.'

'I will tell you from the beginning. I did not intend to worry you, Elizabeth, and all I can say is I'm sorry.'

He took a chair beside the window and started taking off his shoes while Elizabeth grabbed an old newspaper to catch the falling mud.

'I remember walking down the pier with a headache like drums beating non-stop. I decided to get my head under one of those cool waves, so I changed into these clothes, grabbed my trunks and made for the sea.'

'Was that about eleven o'clock?'

Giovanni nodded. 'The cold dip worked wonders. I emerged feeling a new man. It was like a miracle. A marvellous full moon and a gorgeous night. I just set off, walking on and on. It was so quiet, Elizabeth, and I felt at peace with the whole world. I crossed the bridge and in no time I found myself on the Conwy Mountain and making straight on towards Aber.'

He unzipped his anorack and threw it into a corner. Elizabeth waited for him to continue while Gretta made a semblance of starting to lay the tables.

'I got all the inspiration I needed to finish off the slow movement of my symphony. I had my notebook and, the moon being so brilliant, I could get it all down and harmonised. I sat on a rock, I've no idea for how long.'

'And then?'

37

How fascinating it all sounded, Elizabeth thought. Quite 'out of this world' . . .

'I felt this compelling urge to keep going. On and on I walked, mile after mile. Then, quite suddenly, after walking for most of the night, I felt acutely weary, so I dossed down in a convenient barn, half full of quite comfortable bales of hay. When I awoke it was to the sound of the dawn chorus, with the sun full on my face. Jumping off the hay, I pulled myself together and started walking back. With my hopeless sense of location, I wondered if I might get lost. But the sea was my best landmark; as long as I kept that on my left, I would be O.K. And so here I am,' Giovanni shrugged, 'safe and secure within these four walls, with a proper roof over my head.'

There was obvious relief in his face, but more than that, Elizabeth noticed a look of triumph and achievement. She had looked on in stunned silence during his narrative and now it was Gretta who chimed in playfully:

'Really, Gio, if you must be dramatic you do it all wrong. Better if you had them finding you by helicopter or Alsatian dogs with police escort for real drama. What you do, *I* say, is just an anti — anti-climax.' Laughing, she gave him one good push across the kitchen.

Elizabeth was not used to such eccentricities. Life with Roger had been mundane, she knowing his every move and being able to read him like a book. She was quite at a loss to plumb the depths of this extraordinary youngster.

'You must be ravenous,' was all she could think of to say. 'You'll have to be quick to make the concert tonight. Just get washed and changed and then come down for your meal.' How could she scold him? It was his genius in action. Was he not a composer? And did he not live in a world of his own? That he was safe was really all that mattered.

Gio was not hungry. He scarcely ate a thing. He seemed to have lost weight and there was a tired grey look about his face. How much energy he must have expanded during that trek across the hills, Elizabeth reflected as she watched him on the stage that evening, paler and thinner, with a strained nervous look about his eyes. She tried to put it behind her, but it would not go away, this awful nagging feeling that all was not well with Gio.

*   *   *   *

'I say, look at this, you two!'

Gretta was by now getting an excellent grasp of English and she had also helped Elizabeth considerably with her knowledge of German. The 'Weekly Chronicle' was opened out to cover one table and the girl was leaning over it, a dictionary beside her, meticulously working out the meaning of every sentence. The guests had dispersed from the dining room, thrown into their car boots sufficient flasks and lunch boxes to last a month, and were now revving up their engines ready for off. With most of the tables cleared, Gretta felt she deserved a break, particularly as Giovanni had only just taken his place and was tackling his grapefruit.

'Look what it says here,' she repeated. 'All in big letters and lots of colour.'

Elizbaeth was collecting spare rolls, and making sure that Giovanni had a good supply, as Gretta read out in her usual German accent:

' 'Famous T.V. Stars in Spectacular Concert, Wednesday at eight o'clock. Max Ricco, famous guitarist with his fantastic Red Lion Group, top of the pops, supported by world famous organist Frederico Jaffa. Admission four pounds. Book now at Pier Pavilion.' '

Gretta took a breath before adding, with a sparkle in her voice, 'That is marvellous, wunderbar! Music with life in it . . . I will not miss that not for anything. But Mrs. Williams, is it not at the pavilion where you go all the time?'

'No, Gretta dear, Ours is quite small and called the Pier Head Pavilion. That is the big one and holds several thousand.'

'I hope so much that I can get a seat. My friend Heidi will probably come too, and how we shall enjoy it.'

'All right for some, I suppose.' Elizabeth looked dubious: 'There must be a catch in it somewhere. They usually charge over six pounds. Probably a gimmick on the part of the opposition, trying to steal our audiences.'

Gretta wasn't concerned about the opposition: she had no time for classical music. She jumped about in the centre of the room, holding Gio's plate of bacon and eggs high above her head in an attempt to make him laugh.

'There,' she said as she placed it before him. 'Now mind you eat it up, every bit.' And she danced her way out of the room and upstairs.

Elizabeth had started to open her post and was silent for a while. The event Gretta had read out would certainly be a strong counter attraction to Peter's concerts and the arrival of such famous artistes would create a sensation in the town. The four pounds entrance fee must be either a mistake or a bait to get them in.

She sighed and picked up a long white envelope bearing a first class stamp. From London, she noted. As Giovanni watched she pulled out the contents and a cheque fell to the floor.

'Look, Gio,' she exclaimed, radiant now with shining eyes. 'They've accepted those five songs and sent a cheque for £350. Oh, I cannot believe it! I never thought . . .'

Rushing from her corner table, she put her arms round Gio: 'You don't know how grateful I am. It was entirely through your help. Thank you so very much . . .'

'That's all right, Elizabeth. Just keep it up.' He sounded matter-of-fact but his tone was encouraging.

The depressing start to Elizabeth's day was now forgotten. After all these years she had actually sold some songs. A surge of elation swept through her like heady wine as she started up the car and made for the shops. She would get a tonic, she had resolved, to make Giovanni eat more. She'd seen the very thing advertised in the paper the previous day.

As she drove towards the promenade, her eye was caught by a huge coloured poster erected outside the main pier entrance. It was for the Pop Concert, bold and brazen and a real eye-sore. Taking a second look, she gathered from the small print underneath that the four pounds only applied to standing room at the back, the official price being £6. There was a similar boarding just as nauseating, outside the Town Hall.

All kinds of thoughts rushed through Elizabeth's mind. One thing was certain: she must pop in for a chat with Peter. An hour spent over coffee would certainly be an hour well spent.

Chapter 5

It was a warm day, the sun shining brightly from a clear blue sky. Elizabeth felt cool and confident in a new gown of emerald green satin, with flowing sleeves and a low neck-line set off with three rows of cultured pearls and tiny matching ear rings. She did not often spend so much money on herself, but for this occasion she had added a further note of sophistication by piling her hair on top and securing it with a pretty mother-of-pearl clasp.

She received her guests in the spacious hall. Straight from the morning concert, the members of the orchestra arrived with as much hilarity as a load of schoolboys let out to play. Throwing their instruments down in the cloakroom, they were directed towards the lounge, where Naomi and her friend Helen were pouring out sherry and other members of the 'friends' hovered about to act as hosts.

Elizabeth relied on Naomi for her wordly wisdom. She would know which wine to serve, how to seat the guests and when to start the speeches. Naomi's city background had given her a sophistication which, though Elizabeth might never achieve it, remained of invaluable assistance on such occasions as this.

Above the laughter and loud chatter a radiant Elizabeth managed to make herself heard in a cheerful tone:

'It really is good to see you all again at Swallow Tree Gardens — and may I offer a special welcome to our two new members?' She smiled at Sylvia, the new violin player, and Anne. the clarinettist. 'Do please make yourselves thoroughly at home, won't you? Welcome here once again.'

Dr. Emmanual looked most distinguished in a well-cut grey suit, and his spouse had bought a new two-piece in a pale pink

41

nylon to give her broad figure an even fuller appearance. As she greeted her host with a kiss and held out her white gloved hand, Elizabeth wondered momentarily just what Peter had seen in her. The woman had no personality. He was far superior in every way. But perish the thought. She was too well bred to allow herself to dwell upon such ideas.

'Most kind of you, Liz, to invite us all here,' Mrs. Emmanual gushed. 'We do so look forward to this annual event when we see you in your own lovely home.'

'I in turn love to have you,' replied Elizabeth very sincerely. 'The summer season wouldn't be complete without this lunch invitation for the whole orchestra, and these most useful friends to help out.'

'Yes,' Peter chimed in, 'you wonderful ladies deserve a round of applause. As I wave my baton over the heads of these boys and girls and produce many types of musical sounds, I feel that you, as a society, are a great source of strength to us. God bless you all and may you continue to help us during the difficult times ahead.'

Some of the ladies were by now peeping out from behind the red velvet curtain which led to the kitchen, and Peter chuckled as he raised a hand towards them. Then, taking his sherry, he made his way to one of the low comfortable chairs and was soon deep in conversation.

Elizabeth had really 'gone to town' over the meal. She had chosen a day when there were no paying guests, and had promised Gretta an afternoon off. Giovanni had helped most willingly till past midnight in arranging the tables to make one long table down the centre of the dining room. This she had covered with two large white damask cloths, kept for such special occasions, and each of the thirty places was laid with gleaming silver and glittering cut-glass. Each place was labelled by a small parcelled gift, and the snowy white serviettes were folded to look like so many boats about to take off. Flower arrangements of colourful sweet peas and sweet smelling carnations adorned the tables at intervals, and a dozen red candles gave the room the atmosphere of a banquet.

Elizabeth had secured a supply of Scotch salmon and the gardener had produced new potatoes and aspargaus in abundance. This was enhanced by large dishes of fresh green salad, with red peppers and radishes peeping out like flowers on a lawn. Fresh strawberries had also come in from the garden, to be accompanied by the clotted cream which only her milkman could supply. On a side table an exotic cheese-board was displayed, with every conceivable type of cheese and crispbread, and the meal would be rounded off with freshly brewed coffee.

As Elizabeth went towards the kitchen she was surprised to be waylaid by Sylvia. Standing behind the door, the new violinist muttered timidly:

'I hope you won't mind me asking, Mrs. Williams, but I've been looking at the place names on the table . . . Could I possibly change mine over?' Twisting her hankie about, the girl looked as if the whole world depended upon Elizabeth's response.

'Of course, Sylvia. You can sit where you please. But why?'

'You've put me next to Richard . . . the one person who makes me unhappy all the time.'

There were tears in the girl's cornflower blue eyes. Standing there in her pale blue cotton dress, her long blonde hair falling over her shoulders, she made a curiously pathetic figure as she attempted to mop her cheeks with the tiny white hankie.

'All I've done is put you where you sit on the stage,' Elizabeth pointed out.

'Richard is the one I share a stand with, Mrs. Williams, and he's downright horrid to me. He makes me feel inferior somehow.'

'Why ever should he do that?'

'He resents me as a newcomer,' Sylvia quavered. 'The first thing he said to me was that he hates sharing a stand and I'd better keep my bow out of his way.'

'How ridiculous . . .'

'He's always criticising me,' the girl broke in. 'Either I play too loud, or too fast, or I turn over the music too slowly. He — he's beastly to me! I almost feel like leaving . . .'

'Calm down, my dear.' Elizabeth put her arm round Sylvia. 'We can't have tears on a day like this, now can we? I'll do all I can for you and we'll work something out when there's more time. Now let's see what we can carry in from the kitchen. I suggest you sit by me at this end of the table, and then you can stack up the plates as they come along, and pass everything down. How's that?'

'Thank you. You're so kind . . .' Sylvia blew her nose before, putting on a brave face, she joined the crowd again.

43

Lunch was a round of jollity from start to finish. Giovanni was his old self again, a touch of colour in his cheeks as he sat proudly amongst the members of the orchestra as their leader. Always happy-go-lucky and ready for a joke, quick witted and anxious to please, he had gained a number of friends.

Boxes of white handkerchiefs and bottles of after-shave were opened enthusiastically by the boys, with bottles of expensive perfume and pretty lace hankies for the girls. In every case it was clearly just what they wanted. All in all a most extravagant event, but as Elizabeth gazed from face to face, noting Peter's full approval and, in particular, Giovanni's care-free mood, it struck her that never in her wildest dreams would she have imagined a day like this. At that moment it was just perfect in every way. A strong maternal instinct was being satisfied, and it was to her as if her own son was the centre of this luxurious entertainment.

After the meal most of the guests wandered through to the patio and on into the grounds, disappearing amongst the thick colourful rhododendrons. A few made their way down the corridor to Elizabeth's lounge, intending to try out on her piano a new number for the evening concert: a tricky piece, they said, which required a quick going over. The ladies cleared everything away, happy to be of use in such elegant surroundings, and their high pitched prattle could be heard beyond the closed kitchen door.

Mrs. Emmanual had chosen a paper-back from the book-shelf and was making a pretence of reading, but it was obvious to Elizabeth that she was almost asleep. Peter, on his own, beckoned for her to join him in the far corner of the lounge, next to a window overlooking the rose-garden and lawns.

'What's on your mind, Peter?' She took a chair and moved it closer to his.

'I have a problem, Liz dear, as you may have guessed. I've been putting it behind me in the hope it would go away.'

Clearly he had something he wished to get off his chest so she let him continue without interruption.

'It looks, at the moment, as if there may have to be cuts in the number of players.'

'Not that,' Elizabeth breathed, realising she must keep her voice down.

Peter drew on his cigar and puffed out a spiral of blue smoke. His dark eyes held a most worried expression.

'It will be the last resort, of course,' he assured her. 'And we shall do our utmost to avoid such a step. But it is a matter of simple arithmetic, you see, our takings at the door not adding up to the amount I have to pay in musicians' fees.'

'It is a fine orchestra as it is, Peter, and I can't think who we could dispense with. You are such a wonderful conductor too. As for the music, it's beautiful, absolutely out of this world.'

Peter smilingly leaned across to squeeze Elizabeth's hand.

'If only more people in the town thought as you do! You are a real comfort to me, always so understanding when I unburden myself.'

Their eyes met and Elizabeth felt an inner glow: how nice of him to single her out to discuss his problems! He was such an attractive person. As he patted her shoulder, her heart did a quick somersault and left her with a wonderful aura of contentment.

'We've had our share of opposition in the town,' he resumed almost in a whisper. 'Surprising to what lengths some people will go in order to get their own way.'

'Like keeping us waiting outside in the cold and deliberately not opening up until just before starting time.'

'Yes, and failing to open up the bar, the cafe and the kiosks for the use of the audience.'

'True.'

'That pop concert last week drew the crowds and I believe there's another one in the pipeline, a group from Manchester called The Sky Rockets.'

Dr. Emmanual gazed pensively through the window and both he and Elizabeth watched the boys on the lawn, kicking a big red ball about and obviously thoroughly enjoying themselves.

'To decide who would have to go would be a daunting task.' He held out his hand and started counting out his fingers. 'We have to keep six fiddles, four firsts and two seconds. Martin is excellent on the viola. You must have noticed his rich tone. He's essential with the two cellos and Glyn on the bass to boost the lower strings and make a good balance. We can't do without a flute, a clarinet, oboe and horn, just one of each. Russ, on the percussion, keeps a regular beat for us all. Incidentally I admire his xylophone solos — quite exceptional.'

45

Peter paused, then continued with an element of determination: 'That leaves Les, our pianist. He, as you may have noticed, keeps everything going smoothly. If anyone misses his cue, Les it is who thumps it out on the piano, with the audience none the wiser. It happened this morning in *Light Cavalry*.'

He grinned broadly. In an instant their eyes met and both stifled a laugh.

'There is one point you may not have noticed, Peter.'

This, surely, was the moment to mention Sylvia, particularly as he was talking about second violins. Elizabeth still had a vision of her unhappy face just before lunch.

'What's that, then?'

She told the doctor the full story, just as she heard it. An expression of sympathy appeared on his face. In previous years, she gathered, they had managed three second violins, which gave Richard a stand to himself. Fortyish, and a bachelor, he had become selfish and critical, but all the same he was a good strong player who would be missed. Sylvia, though promising and sensitive, was not yet suffiiciently experienced, to be moved over to play first violin. It required great skill to play those high notes on the top of the E string. He had chosen the four first fiddle players because of their perfect intonation. Sylvia, at the moment, would never make it. He also expressed concern over Giovanni: the boy looked rather peaky of late and must not be overworked — they might perhaps cut down on his solos. Both agreed that he had come fully up to expectations and his playing was remarkable.

Elizabeth's eyes lit up as she turned to Peter.

'Look, there's Sylvia walking with Martin just beyond the red rose bushes. And I'm certain he's got his arm round her.'

'Martin, eh? She couldn't find a better chap. He'll look after her. He's my librarian, you know, and can put his hand on a piece of music in a trice.'

It came as a relief to Elizabeth to see Sylvia being taken care of.

The weather held for tea to be served on the lawn, spread out on long tables with the ease and convenience of any self-service buffet. Cucumber sandwiches and sausage rolls were followed by a display of cream cakes of every possible variety. The ice-cream was in mixed flavours of different colours; but the main attraction was a huge cake kept until now behind the scenes and

46

displayed in the centre of the table. One of 'the friends' had created this huge iced spectacle, skilfully shaped like a grand piano with the various instruments of the orchestra professionally worked out in marzipan and scattered over the smooth white surface. The lettering in gold was clearly marked: 'The Palm Court Orchestra — Keep up the Good Work.'

Peter was called on to cut the cake. More sherry was served and loud cheers resounded through the grounds as he made a brief speech of gratitude to Elizabeth and all the helpers.

The last half-hour was as noisy as any children's playground, with much dashing about in and out of the patio doors, some playing wildly on the piano, others trying out recordings and tapes in snatches of tunes. Absolute chaos reigned, and Elizabeth, about to clap her hands and so, hopefully, restore order, heard a heavy tapping on the side window.

Turning quickly towards it, she saw a middle-aged man scowling at her, and, on either side, the faces of an equally sour looking woman and two teenage children. She opened the window to find out what they wanted.

'This is a guest house, I presume, and not a mad-house.' The man's face was red with fury, his tone belligerent. 'I've been hammering on your front door these past ten minutes! Do you realise we're booked in here for two weeks?'

'I don't understand,' faltered Elizabeth, completely taken aback. 'I've nobody booked in for today: I'd kept it free.'

Producing an envelope, he tore it open and thrust it in front of Elizabeth, whose face was by now bright crimson.

'Here it is. Your signature, eh?' he snarled, his face reminding her of that of a huge bull-dog about to attack.

'We're not staying, don't you fret. The mind boggles at such inefficiency. We'll get fixed up in the town.'

With that, and a final glare, he was gone, his family trooping obediently after him towards the car in single file.

A sinking sensation filled the pit of Elizabeth's stomach. How could she have made such a stupid mistake, and on such a day as this? In front of all these lovely people too . . .

As the strange car disappeared from sight, a stunned silence dominated the room. Elizabeth's mind flashed back to her booking chart. Of course — she must have inserted 25th June instead of 25th May! An easy mistake to make when the mind is full of other things.

Then, like a streak of lightning, it dawned on her what an excellent booking it had been — a double and two singles, full board, for two weeks. A loss of over £800 and one which, with the expenses of that day, she could ill afford.

Chapter 6

'Naomi! I must tell you this: it's so important to both of us. That's why I ran to catch you up.'

Elizabeth paused for breath as she faced Naomi on the busy pavement. Her friend was studying a display of mink stoles in the window of the best furrier in town, her auburn hair shaped in an elegant curve and bouncing attractively around her shoulders.

No time in her own active life, Elizabeth convinced herself, for such exotic tastes as mink furs.

'Mind how you go, Liz dear,' Naomi smiled. 'I never saw anyone run so fast along a crowded street! Just relax and tell me slowly what's so important on this beautiful sunny day.'

After a heavy goods vehicle had parked noisily beside the curb, and a local bus had roared by, Elizabeth continued:

'I've seen the agenda for the Council meeting tomorrow night. It's down about Peter Emmanual and his lease of the pavilion.'

'That should be interesting in view of the undercurrent now pervading the town.'

Naomi's eyes widened with concern as Elizabeth rattled on: 'About half the residents are in favour of the concerts and the other half want Peter pushed out.'

'A good chance to find out first hand just what is going on?'

'Well, it's the first item on the agenda so what about meeting me there? We'll make our way to the public gallery like we did before.'

'We're not allowed to make any comments.'

'Oh no! Nor can we vote. The most we *can* do is sit tight and get to know which way the wind's blowing. It's a marvellous chance. Tomorrow night, then, at seven-thirty?'

'Right. I'll see you at the side entrance. We'll go in there and creep up those back stairs.'

*　　*　　*　　*

'How much longer is that treasurer going to be reading his accounts? Here, Liz, have a chocolate.'

Naomi dived into a leather holdall, revealing as she did so a magazine and some knitting.

'Aren't these benches wretchedly hard? Can't see myself coming here very often.'

'Some building scheme by the sound of it.'

Elizabeth tried to sound intelligent, but with difficulty.

'All well above our heads. His figures are in multiples of a thousand.'

'Ah good, he's just sitting down and they've got a proposer and seconder. As soon as they have a show of hands, that boring financial report will have gone through.'

Thirty hands shot up in unison and the chairman's voice boomed around the council chamber like so many low chords on a church organ:

'Carried unanimously, ladies and gentlemen — so we are all agreed that the extension to the Leisure Centre be proceeded with. The next item on the agnda is the question of the lease of the Pier Head Pavilion.'

Within half a minute a stocky middle-aged man rose to his feet. After a quick look towards the chair, he turned his attention to the thirty council members assembled round the polished oak table.

'Fellow members, I would at this stage like to point out that, on January the fourth, a certain proposal was passed by a majority of one, whereas the said proposal would have failed to go through if two of our prominent members had been present.'

His voice was distinctly uneducated, and he continued: 'I refer of course to Zechariah and Idris Jones. I protest that the meeting should have been deferred pending the return of these two gentlemen from their holiday in Austria.'

He sat down heavily with a glow of satisfaction on his flushed face.

The Chairman flicked his bulky Minute Book back a few pages. As he scrutinised the entry for January, another member got up.

'I agree with the previous speaker. That proposal for Dr. Peter Emmanual to lease the Pier Head Pavilion went through on false pretences, and I'll tell you for why. The meeting in January had been pushed forward a week and that is against the constitution. Everybody knows that if Zech and Idris had voted the proposal would never have carried. In short, ladies and gentlemen, the proposal for the Pier Head Pavilion was passed illegally and I, together with many more here tonight, object.'

Caught up with emotion, this second speaker's voice rose and fell with the intonation that only the Welsh can produce.

'The sooner we get rid of that pathetic set-up,' he continued, 'the better it will be for the town! Classical music they call it, but boring it is. There's no beat to it, man. It's just dead. And our town will be dead too if we carry on with such old-fashioned stuff! Get rid of the orchestra, I say, and put a modern dance hall there with flashing lights and disco, pop-group and proper stars.'

Elizabeth caught Naomi's eye as the second speaker sat down, and both frowned in protest. Elizabeth felt a cold shiver pass through her body, and a sensation as if a knife had turned inside her.

'How dare he insult Peter and call our classical music by such names.'

'If this gets in print,' added Naomi, 'poor Peter will be too ashamed to show his face.'

'Don't you believe it,' protested the loyal Elizabeth. 'He'll fight back: he's tougher than he looks. Wait till you hear the other side. That thin man in the navy suit comes to all our concerts. He'll let them have it.'

'Shame on you for making such an accusation.' His voice was rich and mellow and, though Welsh, had a professional ring to it.

'There are two sides to every question, my dear friends. Rash statements should not be made without knowledge of all the facts. Dr. Peter Emmanual has done more than anyone else to retain the good tone of our town. We have long had a reputation for a high standard of entertainment which we intend to keep. Not only that, our visitors can walk peacefully down our promenade any evening, without fear of being molested by gangs of hooligans leaving their rock festivals and late-night discos. These concerts add culture to our town, and I am positive the majority of our

51

residents prefer this to the endless stream of bingo-halls, chippies and slot machines which line other promenades.'

'Rubbish, man. All piffle! Where d'yer think the money's coming from? What we're doing now is throwing rate-payers' hard-earned money down the drain. Till we put a fun fair and disco at the end of that pier, we'll never make a penny out of it. I'm telling you, 'cause I know.'

Several speakers now rose at the same time and the hubbub increased to a crescendo, each one trying to outdo the other. Many members were standing up, waving their arms and shouting without restraint 'disco' . . . 'fun fair' . . . 'slot machines' . . . 'rate-payers' money down the drain'.

'Order! Order, ladies and gentlemen, please!' The Chairman clapped his hands vigorously, his tone as high pitched as any umpire's whistle at the end of a game. 'May I remind you that we are here in this chamber to discuss council business in a calm and efficient way? I have no option, in the circumstances, but to bring this meeting to a premature end: we cannot possibly continue in so uncontrolled a manner. Goodnight, ladies and gentlemen!'

Zechariah Jones had made his name in the town as a wealthy progressive pig farmer, where he and his twenty-five year old son worked daily. It was common knowledge that he could make large profits in his pig rearing capacity, but what was not common knowledge was that he had started out as a qualified veterinary surgeon in South Wales, but quit the area when his name had been struck off the register for illegal and fraudulent dealings in antibiotics, fifteen years before.

He had risen up the ladder of success on the backs of more humble pig farmers, never paying a penny more than was absolutely necessary for his piglets, and always extracting the last pound when it came to selling. He had no conscience and could pull a fast one any time. He had married Gwyneth more for her muscle than her looks, having come across her as a waitress in one of the hotels where he regularly collected his pig food.

The crafty Zechariah made sure that his reputation remained favourable on the surface. He gave generously to good causes if he knew that thereby his name would be blazed around the town. He lived a meagre existence, being almost self-sufficient with his cow, his few hens, his bees and his vegetable patch. As he visited the various farms in the area, on the look out for every piglet he could lay his hands on, he advised farmers in his usual jovial manner, 'You mark my words, that cow has mastitis. I'll get you something that'll cure her for sure,' or 'those heifers show signs of husk' or 'drench those calves with this mixture or you'll get scour and then you'll lose them.'

And so he had gained in popularity, voted in more by his loud voice than by any wisdom or integrity. Each January the three Jones's would spend several hundred pounds on a skiing holiday in the Austrian Alps, Idris indulging in the skiing and his parents in the local pubs. This gave them prestige and something to talk about, and it was during their holiday in January that the fatal meeting of the council had taken place, and the proposition which they so blatantly opposed had gone through by the skin of its teeth. A thousand pounds had already been forfeited on getting Idris a really good drum kit and a set of disco equipment which now filled the whole of the front room and could produce more volume than any express train entering a tunnel. Their ambition now was for Idris to make his name with flashing lights and vibrant music on the end of that pier, and Zechariah looked forward to basking in the reflected glory from his son, and to enjoying a reputation for having saved the town from financial ruin.

Naomi put away her knitting and gathered up the oddments into her bag, while Elizabeth took a last peep over the balcony rail. What looked almost like a fight was going on in one corner of the town hall.

'What a carry on, wasn't it?' Naomi murmured. 'I'd no idea we had such a set of hooligans on our council!'

'These meetings are an eye opener,' Elizabeth nodded. 'And tonight's performance, curtailed though it was, certainly proves just how divided the town is.'

Her tone was one of disgust, but then, as their footsteps echoed along the silent corridor, she added: 'It would be funny, don't you agree, if it wasn't so serious? For entertainment value I reckon it beats TV any time!'

*　　*　　*　　*

It was a particularly hot and sultry night and an influx of visitors in over-sixties coach parties had increased the length

53

of the queue at the Pier Head. It stretched all round the pavilion, meeting up again with itself in a full circle, and the usual hum of conversation grew louder and more excited as more people joined on. The sea below resembled a mill pond and a slight breeze caused a ripple of air to pass between the scantily clad bodies.

The topic of conversation was the chaotic ending to the council meeting of the previous evening. Some of the ladies, with husbands or brothers on the council provided firsthand information, and this was lapped up with all the alacrity of a kitten with a bowl of cream. Trouble was brewing, everyone agreed, and when the adjourned meeting was re-called, another load of criticism would emerge.

It was Gio's solo night. Such evenings were usually a source of great joy to Elizabeth, but tonight he hadn't felt hungry and looked tired. Maybe it was colly wobbles, though, and his butterfly tummy would disappear after his performance. He could always snatch a bite in the interval if he needed it. But it was totally unlike him to be nervous and Elizabeth had felt a twinge of anxiety as he peeped through the kitchen door before leaving the house.

'Sorry, I can't face dinner, Elizabeth. Thought I'd take a stroll around the Marine Drive and get a whiff of fresh air before the concert. I may change that Tarantella and give them a Mozart Minuet and Trio. The fingers get sticky on nights like this and you could lose control on those top notes.'

He'd get his fingers round any piece no matter how fast or high pitched, Elizabeth mused, and Les would follow unerringly with his fantastic accompaniment, just like a cat watching a mouse.

Members of the orchestra, their jackets discarded for the first time this season, looked cool in their usual frilled shirts. Large glasses of iced grapefruit juice were the popular choice during the interval as Elizabeth, followed by Naomi, pushed her way through to join Dr. Emmanual at his corner table. As they reached him he was dropping three lumps of sugar into his coffee and stirring slowly and deliberately.

'In spite of the heat, I prefer coffee,' Elizabeth remarked as Peter made room for the ladies.

The interval was short and whatever was said had to be

brief. Within seven or eight minutes the bell would ring to summon the orchestra back to the stage for the second half.

'Just time to tell you of my scheme, ladies.' There was a sparkle in Peter Emmanual's eye as if he held the key to some enterprise. Elizabeth and Naomi waited expectantly.

'There is a way of drawing the crowds to this pavilion, and the more I think about it the more I'm inclined to try it out, particularly as we have all the advantages of living in Wales.'

He paused, a mischievous smile lurking at his mouth corners as he noted the impression he was making upon his listeners.

'I suggest we organise a Festival of Male Voice Choirs, competing against Ladies' Choirs from all over Wales. Later on we could progress to mixed choirs and children's choirs. Now that, do you not agree, would be a challenge?'

'What a marvellous idea, Peter.' Elizabeth's voice was animated. 'Why didn't we think of it before?' She was as thrilled as if the proposition had been her own.

'The cost need not be high,' Peter continued, 'and any choir worth its salt would be proud to compete. All we need is a few good quality prizes, a silver cup and medal, and the right administration.'

He looked straight at Elizabeth who, with 'organisation' her favourite word, was not slow to take up the challenge.

'Good old Peter,' she enthused. 'I can think of twelve choirs straight off between here and Chester and the other way along the coast to Bangor. Our position is central. We stand to gain from every angle . . .'

At that point the bell rang.

'I'll keep you both informed,' said Peter as he rose from his seat. 'We must draft out a letter for typing and duplicating, and then get it circulated as soon as we can.'

The second half of the concert commenced with the rousing March from *William Tell*, after which the fifteen members walked off stage and Giovanni entered alone to loud applause.

There was something strained about those distinctive features tonight. Elizabeth, ever quick to note any change of expression on the boy's face, was more than a little anxious as he started his first solo. Could there be some worry on his mind or was it just a headache? His customary verve and alacrity were missing and he'd missed his preamble — that story he never failed to include about the Meditation from *Thais* by Massnet. The scene which gave the setting and aroused the emotion of the audience — the girl in the convent forced to give up all ideas of love and romance, and the terrific emotional battle she had with herself when she fell madly in love.

Why was he attacking so delicate a piece with such gusto? Why omit that rallentando? His bow seemed to be gathering speed at every bar! And whatever was he thinking of when he knew full well that passage should be rendered in a broad style at a slow tempo, in order to get the emotional build-up at the end? This was ridiculous! He'd never get through at such a speed! Something was wrong — dreadfully wrong.

Elizabeth could see Les's hands going frantic on the keyboard. He might be phenomenal at following soloists' whims and giving them plenty of scope for self-expression — he wouldn't be able to follow this time. There was a more than uneasy expression on his face. As the seconds passed he began to look desparate. It seemed to Elizabeth that Gio had rushed on, determined to get through the thing as quickly as possible.

Perspiration broke out on her forehead as the youngster attempted a very high note — and failed to reach it. He stopped playing, his bow poised in mid air, and closed his eyes, a grey look now on his pale face. Sick with fright, she twisted her hands in her lap.

After what seemed like hours, but must have been only seconds, his eyes opened as if coming out of a trance, staring dramatically at the ceiling and then around the hall at spellbound faces. Swaying and staggering across the stage, he collapsed in a heap just beneath the foot-lights, his violin and bow flying high into the air and hitting the stage floor a few yards away.

Horrified, unable to move or utter a sound, Elizabeth sat stiff and corpse-like in her seat, staring at poor dear Gio lying in a helpless heap on the stage floor.

The audience gasped. Some rushed forward, a woman screamed and a dog barked. Elizabeth noticed a nurse in blue and white moving in from the crowd and two strong men leaping on to the stage to move the boy to the dressing room.

'I'll bring my car to the stage door . . .' She jerked into action and forced her way through the throng. 'It's nervous exhaustion, the result of all this heat. I'll ring for the doctor as soon as I get him home.'

In the event, it was thirty minutes before Elizabeth could get her car to the end of the pier. Frustration and near despair building up inside her, she had argued and argued with the pier-master for permission to drive on. She felt a shred of confidence as she realised that the nurse and Naomi would be by Gio's side, but as she clenched and unclenched her hands on the steering wheel, jumbled and tortured images of the unconscious boy kept appearing in her mind.

'He's come round now,' the nurse assured her. 'Far from well, however. I've taken his pulse and his temperature and I think we should take him to the hospital. His breathing is too rapid for my liking.'

The Emergency Department at the hospital was particularly quiet. What seemed like hours passed as Elizabeth and Naomi sat in the corridor waiting for news. There were endless questions, and a white-coated house-man wrote everything down. She gave Peter as next of kin, the Social Services having agreed at the beginning of the season to leave Gio's career in the doctor's capable hands. She mentioned his head-aches and his lack of appetite. She knew very little of his background, she explained, and many questions remained unanswered. She made a mental note to get in touch with that tutor of his who had been his good friend for several years, and the children's home in Manchester would furnish his entire case history.

'Cheer up, Liz darling.' Naomi, optimistic as ever, gave her a hug and a big smile. 'He'll be home tomorrow, large as life and just as cheeky! They're only keeping him in to keep an eye on him and your guest house is hardly the place for him at the moment.'

The Sister allowed them to peep at Gio as he lay semi-conscious in a bed at the end of the ward. The clock in her office was coming up to eleven o'clock. Various tests were being taken and it would be at least twenty-four hours before any results were known. It could be a severe case of nervous exhaustion, Sister pointed out, due to overwork and under-nourishment, and she advised Elizabeth to telephone first thing in the morning.

The phone was ringing as Elizabeth swung into the drive and she saw Gretta rushing past the window to answer it. The German girl had kept everything going most efficiently in the lounge, the hot drinks being served in Elizabeth's absence.

'It is Dr. Emmanual, Mrs. Williams! Urgent it sounds. Half an hour ago he also phone.'

Breathless with hurrying, Elizabeth grabbed the receiver.

'Peter? I was about to phone you. Isn't it awfully worrying? They've kept him in at the hospital!'

'The best place for him, my dear. They will find out precisely what is wrong and let us know.'

Peter had other problems on his mind. After thanking Elizabeth for all her efforts, his voice faltered as he went on:

'I've had such a dirty trick played on me. You know Clara and I sometimes walk on fine nights. We did so tonight, leaving the Volvo in the garage behind the house — and you'll never guess what's happened. Our lovely car was vandalised in our absence.'

'Oh no . . .'

'Some hooligans broke in, stripped the car of its wheels and daubed red paint all over the bodywork. In the horrible graffiti it says — 'GET STUFFED DOCTOR — MAKE WAY FOR OUR DISCO'.'

'The rotters,' gasped an appalled Elizabeth. 'How could they do such a wicked thing? This sounds like the work of Idris Jones and his pals.'

Chapter 7

Peter Emmanual's visit to the police station was as frustrating as it was lengthy. While sympathising with him over the damage to his car, the Chief Constable could be of very little help as there was no witness at the scene and nothing suspicious had been reported in the area at that time. All details were taken down and he promised the case would be followed up, also advising Peter to contact his insurance company. The whole episode left a nasty taste behind it, and Peter, usually good natured, became irritable every time the subject was mentioned. He felt the police could do more to help him if they tried, and, to put it mildly, bitterly resented this blow to his pride.

Elizabeth took him in her car to the hospital the following day. Both were intensely relieved to find Giovanni sitting beside his bed in dressing gown and slippers, reading a magazine.

Jovial as usual, Peter was first to speak. 'Who's a naughty boy then? That was a dramatic scene, you falling all over my stage. Shame on you for giving us such a fright!'

'Sorry, sir.' Giovanni grinned, enjoying the doctor's joke. 'I went out like a flame with no warning at all. One minute I was playing that Meditation much too fast — the next, it seemed, I was in here.'

'How do you feel now?' Elizabeth chimed in, holding his warm hand in hers. 'Is there anything you need?'

'Nothing, thanks. I'm very comfortable and they're very kind to me. You know,' he continued, half smiling, 'this reminds me of the San. at the children's home. Some of the kids used to fake illness to miss lessons. It was so very cosy in the San. and that's how it feels here.'

All three laughed, and then Elizabeth, glancing surreptitiously at the temperature chart at the foot of Gio's bed, only half listened as Peter chatted away to the boy.

The lunch trolley appeared at the top of the ward, and both got up to go.

'We'll soon get you out of here, my boy. I'll have a word with Sister.'

Before they left Elizabeth was pleased to see Gio starting on a bowl of thick chicken soup with an appetising smell. After a few words of affectionate assurance, she followed Peter down the ward.

The clinical smell of polish and anaesthetic brought curious sensations to Elizabeth and her legs felt like jelly as she and Peter moved towards Sister's office. Haunted by memories of hospital procedure five years ago, she felt a spasm of pain and loss, as if part of her own body were being torn away.

'Remember, Liz, he's young and virile,' said Peter, noticing her tears. 'I've seen it happen before, a young soloist becoming all strung up. In the end their nerves give way. He's been doing far too much lately and we must make sure he gets all his strength back before we tax his brain any more.'

Sister proved rather detached: 'We've taken a number of tests and a few X-rays, and some of these tests have proved negative. There is, however, some deficiency in the red corpuscles of his blood and the doctor has recommended that we transfer him to Liverpool Walton for further tests.'

Misty tears blurred Elizabeth's vision. Peter asked further questions and she vaguely heard some of the answers. Giovanni would be taken to Liverpool by ambulance soon after lunch, she gathered, and remain there for three days at least.

Elizabeth forced herself to concentrate on the drive home through heavy traffic, with Peter continuing his efforts to cheer her out of her depression:

'You're over-reacting again, my dear. He's going to be all right. It'll be for the best in the long run, I'm sure. His favourite tutor lives somewhere in this district and if I give him a ring he'll certainly visit him there. This worrying isn't like you and you must tell yourself — and believe it — that everything will be back to normal in no time.'

But Elizabeth's feelings of apprehension persisted. If Giovanni was all right, why couldn't he come home? And why Liverpool of all places? All very well for Peter, her thoughts ran on. He'd never had children so how could he appreciate the anguish of a mother over the illness of a child? His baby was his mauve Volvo car and his affection for that was all too obvious; why, he was making as much fuss about it as a child deprived of a favourite toy!

Arriving home to an empty house, she made herself a cup of tea and sat in the lounge, trying to watch television. Her eyes did not focus on the screen, and within an hour she was in the kitchen, restless and halfhearted as she prepared the evening meal.

*   *   *   *

It was Wednesday night again — the night which should have included Gio's solos.

Sylvia surveyed the rows of blurred faces hardly visible against the footlights. She remembered Martin's words — 'Never think of the audience as people criticising you, but instead as rows and rows of cabbages. Then your nerves will disperse like Autumn leaves on a windy day.'

Against all expectations she had pulled it off, her clear soprano voice remaining steady and bell-like throughout the three operatic arias. From Dr. Emmanual's smile of approval she knew she had given a first-class performance.

Sylvia looked radiant in pale blue, long and flowing, trimmed with sequins. A pink sash emphasised the trimmes of her waist and her beautiful blonde hair fell about her shoulders exaggerating her youth.

Elizabeth, in the front row, was as pleased and surprised as everybody else, applauding loud and long when the girl took her bow for the second time.

Dr. Emmanual, quick to replace Giovanni on his solo night with someone equally young and attractive, had been overjoyed on hearing from Martin that Sylvia had taken voice production as her second subject at college. Her voice was excellent, Martin had continued, and at his suggestion she had been taking elocution lessons to help overcome her nervousness.

Peter was always keen to display youthful talent: in fact he tended to avoid bald heads and wrinkled faces on his stage, knowing the public's preference for a pretty face, a youthful figure and plenty of hair. When such assets as these were com-

61

bined with musical excellence, Peter stepped in. That night Sylvia had rendered her solos with all the expertise of a true professional and there and then Peter had decided that full use must be made of this talented young beauty who looked so adorable in her pale blue gown.

It had taken Sylvia years to conquer her inferior complex. She had been up against it most of her life, but especially at school and college. The middle child in a family of five, with two older sisters and two younger brothers, she was always the one left out of everything, too young to be allowed privileges, too old to be made a fuss of.

There were few treats in that house as money was scarce, and Sylvia was expected to contribute to the family income as a thirteen year old papergirl and later on as a part-time waitress in a cafe. At school she would have given anything to have made a break-through and come out with flying colours, but she never did. Her exam results were no more than average and she never excelled at games or played for the school. Her best friend was head girl and both her sisters form captains — but, try as she would, nothing like that came Sylvia's way.

The verses and articles she wrote for the school magazine were never published, although she had sat up all night with a view to making them interesting and readable. How she would have loved to have seen her name in print, or to have had a medal or certificate to show what she was worth. In the school orchestra she was always placed at the back out of sight, whilst, as everyone knew, those at the front got all the praise. The serious boys avoided her, having been warned that all blondes were empty headed. And when she did get a date, the conversation didn't interest her, centring as it did around pop music and sport.

Sylvia and Martin had been on intimate terms since the lunch party at Swallow Tree Gardens. Even before that, she had admired him for his intervention when Richard had lectured her about the speed at which she was playing.

'You're wrong there, Richard,' Martin had chipped in with authority. 'Sylvia's tempo is just about right. The fault was yours, taking the thing too fast. You were a full half beat in front of the others.'

Sylvia had been delighted that someone should have come to her aid — and particularly the handsome Martin with his pleasant smile and kind voice. Unknown to the rest of the orchestra, they had visited each other's flats for lunch or tea, and their friendship had developed. Sylvia would buy ingredients for a fruit cake and take it along to Martin's flat, where they would enjoy endless cups of coffee. Only that week she had made an apple pie with sultanas and cinnamon and they had talked for hours over the lunch table.

She seemed to be able to tell him just about anything, she admitted to herself. Never had she felt like this about anyone. He knew exactly what she wanted out of life. If she told him about her lack of confidence, perhaps he could help her . . .

'What you need, my love, is a dose of my father's Pelmanism. The only thing I know for bolstering up confidence. That course put me right years ago.'

Martin had looked lovingly into Sylvia's innocent blue eyes, vowing to do his utmost to give her that touch of assurance she so badly needed, no matter how long it took.

'Nothing succeeds like success,' he had emphasised. 'And once you've turned the corner and started to win instead of lose, you'll never look back.'

He had explained about the formula his father had drummed into him, the auto-suggestion which had to be repeated daily to convince yourself that every day in every way you were gaining confidence. It sounded easy enough, and the long country walks and deep breathing exercises would be fun. All in all, she decided, it was a case of hypnotising oneself into a feeling of security, dispelling all thoughts of failure and inferiority and replacing them with positive thoughts of success.

'I know someone who'll teach you deportment and elocution.'

Martin was as excited as Sylvia as they arranged the programme of exercises and realised that an improvement had already set in.

He taught her to drive.

'Anyone who takes a car on these busy roads in the summer has to be self-confident,' he had enthused as he fastened the 'L' plates into position and took his place in the passenger seat for the first time.

'And something else, my sweet.' His tone had been rich with encouragement. 'You'll not be playing second fiddle much longer. A pal of mine is selling his viola and I've made him an offer. It's an easy transition from violin to viola and I can soon let you into the secrets of the alto clef and the mysteries of the 'C' string.'

'Well, I don't know . . .'

Martin had waved her doubts aside: 'It's an easier instrument to play. You only get a quarter of the notes the first fiddles get, and none of those high squeaky notes everybody finds difficult. You can hear yourself playing, in that lovely mellow tone, sitting by the cellos, and you won't be a bit sorry now, will you, to get away from Richard and join our crowd in the bass section?'

She already felt a different person, Sylvia realized, and it wasn't only this Pelman System; no, it was the loving way Martin looked at her, his consideration and his enduring affection. She admired his kind brown eyes, his smooth olive skin and that roguish neat black beard of his. With his strong arm around her, protective and caring, she got a delicious feeling of ecstasy she'd never before experienced.

On an impulse Martin had suggested to Dr. Emmanual that Sylvia might take Giovanni's solo night. He had taken her to the boutique, scrutinised everything she tried on, and finally paid for the blue nylon gown with matching shoes. She had felt exactly like a princess being fitted out for a ball.

To play safe she had chosen three solos she'd sung for her finals at college which were still fresh in her memory. Now, all had the quality of a dream as she stood on stage, surveying her captivated, still clapping audience. So she'd finally done it: she really was a success! There was Elizabeth smiling at her. And Dr. Emmanual looked like a king on a throne in all his glory, with that radiant smile and beaming face.

Leaving the stage for the third time, Sylvia rushed straight into the arms of Martin, who held her close as he congratulated her. She felt happy in those moments as never before.

Sylvia entered her dressing room to exchange her smooth nylon dress for the black and white smartness of an orchestral member. As she glanced at the sparkling sequins on her gown, it seemed to her as if they were smiling up at her, congratulating her on her success.

Thank you, Martin darling, she murmured. Now I know for sure that my days of playing second fiddle are numbered. People are going to notice me — and, with you at my side, I'm going to be a somebody at last.

Chapter 8

'You know, Liz, I'm coming round to liking this classical stuff of yours.'

Roger was glancing through Elizabeth's record catalogue and, at the same time, tucking into his bacon and eggs as if it was the best meal he had tackled for weeks.

'Great — you've got Tchaikovsky's *1812 Overture!*' he exclaimed. 'The pal I share digs with plays that morning and night. He must be addicted to it, and I know every note! Certainly gets exciting towards the end.'

It was seven o'clock and Roger, home for a few days, had a fishing trip planned. Too early to start the visitors' breakfasts so Elizabeth was making sure he had a good start for the day and an ample packed lunch to last him till the evening. It was with a feeling of satisfaction that she busied herself in the kitchen. Something that had been missing for a long time was now, she felt, taking shape.

'The *1812* is a fine overture,' she replied, 'but rather ambitious for our orchestra, Roger, you need lots of brass for the effects.'

She was delighted to hear him passing complimentary remarks about her music. He must have changed a good deal. With the hospital project at Jedda coming to an end, he would soon be transferred back to Head Office at Wrexham, only fifty miles away, and could then come home more often.

'I had thought of popping along with you to one of your concerts.'

There was a newfound animation in his voice and a sensation of joy passed through her as he spoke. The least she could do would be to encourage him in his liking for good music. And how lovely it would be to have him sitting beside her at the pavilion!

'I can tell this young fiddle player means a lot to you,' Roger went on. 'You've looked years younger since he first came here at Easter and you seem altogether happier somehow.'

'I *was* happy until three weeks ago, Roger,' Elizabeth replied, 'when the poor kid had this nasty turn. Now it's one long worry, wondering what's wrong with him and when he'll be coming home. The doctors seem mystified. They say his legs have swollen and he's complaining of a pain in his left side.'

'That could be side effects from the drugs they're giving him, or maybe he's allergic to something. Aren't you seeing him tomorrow?'

'Yes, I'm taking Peter along and we hope to see the consultant. We shall make an early start; Peter has to get back in time for his concert, and there's my evening meal. The traffic always builds up near the tunnel, so we must avoid the rush hour.'

How glad I'll be when it's all over, she thought. If only they would tell us what's wrong. It's not knowing that is so worrying. If only I knew, I'd be happier.

'I know how you feel, luv,' said Roger quietly, as if she had spoken aloud.

Elizabeth finished cutting up the bacon and laid it in rows across the grill pan. She counted out eighteen eggs, then took the seat beside Roger and poured a second cup of tea.

'You know, Roger,' she began in a voice full of emotion, 'we're not too old to have a child of our own.'

He looked startled at this bolt from the blue, his expression that of a man caught suddenly off guard.

'If that's what you want, Liz, I'm not against it. But — haven't you enough on your plate with all these visitors, and all this music?'

'People can always make time for the things they really want. Actually, I'm not that keen on the medical side of it . . . all that pregnancy stuff.' Elizabeth grimaced and screwed up her nose. 'All the same, it would be nice to have a child around again to teach things and be responsible for.'

'If that is what would make you happy, so be it,' Roger smiled. 'We're neither of us old really, are we? I've seen women of forty pushing prams round here. To change the subject, Liz, I was awfully chuffed about you selling those songs. And what a cheque! This Giovanni is obviously quite an asset. For years I saw you scribbling on bits of manuscript paper and never having any luck, and as soon as he comes along you get five songs published straight off. It's marvellous: tell him so from me!'

Clearly jubilant, Roger collected his fishing tackle, his flask of coffee and his lunch box and set off for the day.

'By the way,' he shouted before he left, 'I heard a rumour in the pub last night that Idris and his pop group were responsible for the damage to the doctor's car and they're gloating over it because nothing's happened to them. Now they're planning another coup.'

'Another coup,' Elizabeth echoed, her heart giving a lurch of dismay. 'Whatever do you know, Roger? If you tell me we can at least be prepared. We may even forestall them.'

'Two fellas overheard Idris and his friend boasting about being able to drown Dr. Emmanual in more ways than one, and saying that this time they intended to pull all the stops out. Also, Idris told a woman who buys her eggs there that he and his group were determined to take over the pier head — even if it meant pushing Peter Emmanual over the rails and into the sea.'

'What a dreadful thought,' Elizabeth faltered. 'Oh, it's too horrible for words . . .'

'Don't take it too literally, luv. Only a rumour, remember, and people are prone to say anything at all after a few drinks.'

With that Roger was gone, leaving Elizabeth shocked and puzzled. How on earth were they to watch out if they had no idea where or when the attack would come? It really was quite frightening.

A satisfied Roger swooped into the kitchen at five o'clock holding three large mackerel and one large skate. After their meal, to Elizabeth's delight, he referred again to the evening concert and seemed determined to go.

She felt ten feet tall as they walked the length of the pier with her arm in his. It was a wonderful boost to her ego to have her man walking at her side. How smart he looked in his pale grey suit and pink shirt. And his aftershave tonight was particularly subtle. She was reminded strongly of carefree days when they had gone out regularly together.

Quiet waves were washing the beach and salty smells of sea weed hung on the air. It had been a warm day, but now a pleasant breeze stirred as they plodded further out to sea along the wooden slats of the pier.

'It's a Viennese Night, Roger,' Elizabeth volunteered, her

67

voice cheerful and encouraging. 'They'll be playing Strauss waltzes you probably know quite well. Did I tell you Peter has brought out his violin?' she added. 'He hasn't bothered to replace Gio. He stands up and plays the leads as well.'

'Like Max Jaffa, you mean, waving his bow about?'

'Something like that,' she replied pleasantly and both laughed. Then Roger looked anxious:

'You know, seeing all these youngsters about makes me rather suspicious. One of my reasons for coming along tonight was that rumour in the bar. I hate to think of you being involved in some sort of punch-up.'

Elizabeth nodded. 'It might be a coincidence, Roger, but there *are* more young people about. It usually looks like a pensioners' outing on the pier about this time.'

It was an excellent programme and Roger was keen to applaud after the first half. He agreed with Elizabeth that the first row gave a fine view of all the instruments: from that position there were no distractions; no heads bobbing about in front of one. During the interval the cafe was over full with noisy young people devouring cokes, crisps and hamburgers.

Several people enquired about Giovanni but Elizabeth could not give much information. Every day, when she phoned, the Sister supplied the usual 'as well as can be expected', and what could be more vague or infuriating? Everyone, to her pleasure, had a word for Roger, and Peter in particular singled him out. But of course he was always pleased to know there was an extra admirer in his audience.

The second half started with several Struass favourites, and two really exotic cello solos followed. The hall was always full for these Viennese Nights and this audience seemed unusually appreciative.

Peter announced the next item and, with a flourish of his bow, led the orchestra in on a slow cantabile theme. The volume increased as the movement developed. Suddenly a loud reverberating noise made everybody sit bolt upright and turn their heads towards the door. The sound seemed to come from the direction of the cafe, booming away with deafening ear-splitting crashes.

As all eyes turned towards the side windows it became obvious who was responsible. The cafe had been transformed into a concert hall, tables stacked one above the other to make a provisional stage on which apparatus had been set into motion cleverly and secretly without arousing suspicion. Row upon row of teenagers were clearly visible, clapping their hands and stamping their feet in rhythm to the vibrating boom of Idris and his pop group.

How absolutely disgusting, thought Elizabeth as Roger's words flashed through her mind. Hadn't someone said there were more ways of drowing Peter Emmanual than actually pushing him off the pier? Never in all her life had she heard such a jarring, nauseating sound! She knew pop groups were noisy but this was too overpowering for words, completely blotting out the strains of the orchestra.

Roger sprang up and left by a side door, but not before he had shouted to Elizabeth, 'I'm phoning the police from the bar! This doesn't surprise me one bit. What's more, I know how to handle this kind of thing.'

Elizabeth felt relieved that at least Roger had jumped so promptly into action. How dare they do such a detestable thing! Why, they were desecrating Peter's music! Obviously this was part of their campaign to disrupt the lovely concerts and take over the pavilion for themselves.

She could see from the opposite window that Roger had entered the bar and made for the kiosk. Getting up, she leaned over the potted geraniums and shouted to Peter: 'Roger is in touch with the police.' The doctor nodded. Clearly embarrassed by the disturbance, he was wiping his brow with a handkerchief and the orchestra members were exchanging confused, helpless glances. The audience had become restless and irritated, some openly complaining. It seemed evident that the interruption had been designed to ruin the last three items on the Viennese programme, and as the orchestra finally gave up in disgust and most of the audience stood up in protest, it looked as if the opposition had succeeded.

'Ladies and gentlemen, I must apologise for this interruption to our concert,' Peter shouted above the commotion. 'Thanks to the prompt action of Mr. Roger Williams, however, we shall not be called upon to tolerate this nuisance much longer: he has contacted the police. I urge you all to sit down and remain inside this pavilion until you are told to go. May I suggest that you chat sociably together to fill in the time?'

Roger had by now returned to his place. Moments later, everyone was relieved to hear a police car zoom towards the cafe entrance. Four hefty policemen leapt out, followed by four smart

69

policewomen, and made short work of disrupting the rival performance, in all its glory, the punk hairdos and painted faces. Within ten minutes, Idris' expensive equipment had been bundled into his van and a crowd of noisy, boisterous youngsters was being shepherded the length of the pier by the policewomen.

The kids had had their evening. With a warning and a threat the disturbance had been terminated — but the effect was still there. Peter Emmanual felt ruefully that the opposition had scored a point. His Viennese Night had been completely ruined, and an even fouler taste left behind them.

*　　*　　*　　*

'I'm so glad you managed to come, Mrs. Williams and Dr. Emmanual. Giovanni Malvolio . . . a sad case indeed.'

The hospital consultant was studying the pink medical file. Immaculate in his navy suit, his shiny bald patch visible as he looked down at the relevant papers, he was seated behind an oak desk in the thickly carpeted consulting room. Elizabeth and the doctor sat opposite him, too far away for Elizabeth to be able to decipher what he was studying. She was aware that the man must be well used to interviews such as this, hardened, in fact, to imparting news about illnesses. And this was the moment she had been waiting for. Expect the worst, she told herself, yet hope for the best, and really listen carefully . . .

'As you know,' he began, 'we've made a number of tests and also X-rayed the area around the liver and the spleen. We find a distinct enlargement of the spleen with cirrhosis of the liver, which accounts for the pain and swelling in the left side of the feet.'

Elizabeth remained silent, leaving Peter to remark in a low serious tone:

'What does that imply, doctor?'

'A form of leukaemia, at a rather advanced stage, I fear. The cause in most cases is malnutrition — in Giovanni's case of quite long-standing. The boy is under-nourished and this has probably been building up for years. However, heredity cannot be ruled out. These weaknesses do run in families.'

The consultant turned over the pages in the file and held up the X-ray to the light. Her heart dropping like a stone, Elizabeth forced herself to concentrate as he turned towards her.

70

'What this means, Mrs. Williams, is that in Giovanni's case the number of red corpuscles is far out-numbered by the number of white ones. It is virtually a case of splenic anaemia, also known as Bontis Disease. The red corpuscles are not being replaced, and so the blood is starved and anaemic.'

Cold all over now, Elizabeth looked across at Peter, whose face had dropped. The monotonous voice continued, efficient and business-like, yet tempered with a degree of compassion:

'I'm afraid it is very serious in this particular case. Removal of the spleen, where this is possible, may give a fifty-fifty chance of survival.'

Elizabeth was trembling all over. 'There — there must be something you can do for him! Surely there is some hope? If — if we had a second opinion . . .?' Her voice had broken on the last word as her eyes filled with tears.

'No, Mrs. Williams. This complaint is terminal I regret to say.'

Clearly the consultant was making his point as kindly as he could in these tragic circumstances. 'There is no cure for this type of leukaemia, the disease is too far advanced.'

Desolation filled Elizabeth's heart. Her mind in a turmoil, a sickly sensation in her stomach, she heard Peter's voice and it sounded far away:

'How long do you give him? Is there any way of telling?'

'It is most difficult to be precise, Dr. Emmanual. Six months, I would say, although it could be nine, even a year.'

This couldn't be true: surely it was a nightmare from which she would soon awake? Elizabeth's heart began to race, forcing the blood to her head, as the consultant stood up, closing the file. She and Peter also got to their feet.

'You have my sympathy, both of you, and it was good of you to come all this way. My only regret is that I could not offer you a more encouraging verdict.'

He shook hands with each of them, then ushered them to the door.

'I would suggest that you take Giovanni home, tell him gently of the position, and make sure that he gets the finest quality of the life that remains to him.'

The days had been long for Giovanni in hospital, with plenty of time for contemplation. Why was Elizabeth so keen to give him everything he wished for? As soon as he got back to Swallow Tree Gardens she would be fussing around him, checking on whether

71

he had everything he needed. She enjoyed his playing and derived such pleasure from having him around. Well, he could keep up the playing as long as she wished to hear it. What else did he have to offer? It was cushy being looked after and indulged and life at Swallow Tree Gardens was a revelation after his previous existence. Why, Elizabeth treated him like her own son! One day, he had resolved, he would do his level best to repay her. She often told him that fame would be his if he continued to plod on. Well, then would be the time for him to repay her. This was the first time in his life he'd been made a fuss of and he certainly wasn't going to refuse that. Surely he was entitled to a bit of home comfort, a bit of praise, of motherly affection? But he would definitely give Elizabeth something to be proud of — one day.

Elizabeth made desperate efforts to get herself to think straight. Unthinkable, she reasoned, that the life of such a promising young man should be so curtailed. Where was the justice? Never in her life had she met such an unassuming, unconceited person. Gio never talked about himself; she had to prise it out of him. Preposterous that his life should end like this. What possible cause could be served by his death at twenty?

And all the time, she pondered sadly, she'd had visions of him appearing on the concert platforms of the great cities, touring with one of the London orchestras, playing concertos to massive audiences. She had visualized him at thirty at the very height of his career, with his name on all the best programmes and his face emblazoned on all the television screens; and later on as a composer perhaps, with at least one symphony to his credit.

So often those big black eyes of his stared into space, making her wonder what was going on in that profound mind. And when their eyes met he smiled quietly, as if caught off-guard. But she spoke the same language. Of who else could she ask a stupid question and get a sensible answer? Every point that had baffled her in the past about the mysteries of music Giovanni had clarified from his vast storehouse of knowledge. His brain was a computer, fed all along with musical know-how. How utterly unreasonable it seemed that he should not live to enjoy the success she had so hoped for him.

Thus did Elizabeth fight with her whole being what seemed to be the inevitable. She would move Heaven and Earth to help her poor Gio, who did not even know, as yet, his probable fate. And she had the unenviable task of breaking the news to him.

Chapter 9

Next morning Elizabeth spent some time in the reference library, studying the pages of *Gray's Anatomy*. It made depressing reading. She soon realised that the terms 'leukaemia' and 'cancer' were so closely related that the hospital's verdict might well be right. She would nevertheless have a long talk on the subject with her own doctor and push for a second opinion.

At home she stared out of the window but saw nothing. A dear aunt of hers had died of cancer several years before, but at over sixty, with a good life already behind her. This poor boy, not yet twenty, was already sentenced to death. What a dreadful waste of talent it seemed — totally undeserving, totally unjust.

Elizabeth also recalled, when she was quite young, a child of three who had a rare blood group and caused real anxiety to his parents. She remembered the various blood transfusions he had undergone, recovering only for short periods, and she could still visualise the stricken look on his parents' faces when he had died the following year.

Giovanni was such a dear boy, and how happily he had made his home at Swallow Tree Gardens. His music had permeated the house and there would be a dreadful gap in her life when it was no longer there. Halfway through the morning she put on the kettle for a cup of tea, wishing with all her heart that Roger was there, so alone did she feel.

Peter Emmanual was shattered and despondent. He, like Elizabeth, could hardly believe it to be true. As the news leaked out at the Pier Head, the concert audience were deeply grieved, and there were tears and long faces in the cafe during the interval when Elizabeth told them what she knew.

For the first three days Giovanni went to pieces. Apparently

73

in a trance, he remained in his room for long periods, cutting himself off from everybody. In the mornings he said he felt too miserable to get up and stayed in bed till noon, ignoring the breakfast tray.

'It's such a terrific shock, Elizabeth . . . it doesn't add up. It can't be true, can it? That fellow must have made a mistake . . .' As he stirred his coffee, Giovanni searched Elizabeth's face for some measure of reassurance. She got up to draw the curtains. It wasn't really dark but somehow she longed to shut out that cold world outside, and enjoy to the full Gio's cosy warmth and affection. Before very long he wouldn't be here: how could she ever face the fact?

'There were so many things I wanted to do, Elizabeth.' He stared wistfully at the pattern on the carpet. 'I've always struggled to express myself with my playing, and on paper, but I've never felt so much at peace as I have here with you.'

His left hand rose towards the ceiling in a gesture which seemed to embrace the whole house. Elizabeth noted the mature expression on his face as he took another gulp of his coffee. Then he continued:

'You give me courage, because you listen to what I play. Nobody else ever bothered. It's as if your mind goes along with mine. This house has everything I need: peace, quiet, goodness . . . If only you knew how you've helped me.'

His voice had broken into a sob. Replacing his empty cup, he covered his face with both hands and his body seemed to crumple.

'You must be brave, Gio,' Elizabeth said quietly, as she stroked his head. 'There's one whole year for you.' She was being optimistic and she knew it.

'Yes, I know . . . It still hasn't sunk in properly. It's like a bad dream where I'll wake up to find everything normal again.'

But that was the awful part: It wasn't a dream at all. The whole idea was too dreadful to contemplate and her job was to try and keep this boy as happy as possible for the time remained.

Gretta communicated best. She it was who coaxed the invalid to eat morsels of nourishing food, beating up eggs with milk and brandy, and going out specially to buy some of his favourite foods. Everything was served on an attractive tray with a tiny posy of fresh flowers. Elizabeth noted the look of dedication with which Gretta regularly crept upstairs either merely to check on him or to offer yet another tempting dish of her own making. What a great comfort she must be to him at this time. She reminded Elizabeth of an angel of mercy with that noncommittal smile on her face.

Quite unexpectedly, after eight days of almost complete solitude, Giovanni appeared in the kitchen one evening, just before midnight, as Elizabeth was clearing everything away. He pulled out one of the high stools from under the serving table, then seated himself and folded his arms, with an ethereal look about his upturned face.

'This depression thing has gone on too long, Elizabeth, and I intend to change it all!'

Too startled at first to answer, she let him continue in the same decisive tones:

'O.K., my life has been shortened — but I'm still here and have my faculties. I intend to finish my symphony, Elizabeth, and to master the Elgar Concerto.'

She could have wept with emotion. Instead she replied with all the enthusiasm she could muster:

'Good for you, Gio. I admire your attitude and your courage. And now it all comes back to me. Remember our first proper conversation on your first night here?'

'Of course I do!' Some of the old confidence had filtered back into his voice. 'I shall never forget that exhilarating talk of ours, when I confided to you all my hopes and ambitions. You are the most understanding person I know.'

His tone was wistful and faraway, his expression thoughtful. Elizabeth was delighted to see such a transformation in so short a time. Was it the cortisone working? She had almost forgotten the array of tablets he had been given, some to ease the pain, others to keep up his spirits and overcome the depression.

He was still talking, with intense animation now and a certain radiance about his features. Pulling out another stool, she sat beside him.

'As I say,' he continued, 'I shall proceed with my ambitions. I shall work on the last movement of my symphony and then present the whole thing to Doctor Emmanual, in the hope he'll get it performed and I may hear it myself.'

It dawned on Elizabeth at this moment that there was another ambition, quite apart from the symphony and the Elgar Concerto. It was a desire he had not mentioned since. More than anything in the world, he had said, he would like to possess an authentic Italian violin.

She had read about these violins. Hand-made by the old Italian craftsmen in Cremona, they sold at thousands of pounds. Here indeed was a challenge! The money was there in the current account: twelve thousand pounds, intended for the central heating. It had struck her like a shaft of light in a dark forest. What was the use of all that money standing in the bank when this boy, deprived of life, needed a genuine Italian violin? The central heating could wait! Hadn't the house carried on well enough without it all these years? Giovanni should have his violin, and the only way to achieve this objective was for them both to make a trip to London, to that reputable dealer in Wardour Street whom she knew quite well.

The first through train to Euston started at six in the morning. Elizabeth gave full instructions to Gretta about breakfast. She had no qualms about this; the visitors would be catered for and she would be back in time to prepare the evening meal. Meanwhile Gio would get his violin.

The boy's philosophical approach had caught on. True, it was the quality of life that mattered, not the quantity. The boy was right. Hundreds of people lived humdrum lives which drifted on for seventy years or more, but he was determined to make the very best possible use of the short time allotted to him. Yes, he would ride out the storm, shape out his time, and not one second would be wasted.

The train journey was uneventful. Elizabeth had made sure Giovanni brought his tablets with him, and an extra wooly just in case, but he didn't seem to need them. The rattle of cups and plates and the appetising aroma of cooked breakfast attracted them into the dining car, where they enjoyed a fry-up of sausages, gammon, eggs and beans. With his appetite regained, she noted happily, Gio even ordered extra toast.

A taxi swept them across the city to the Wardour Street premises and Elizabeth experienced a wonderful feeling of elation as they crossed the threshold of this world-famous violin dealer.

She would never forget the three hour session in their studio. It all passed too quickly, and she was captivated as Gio tried out each of the many rare instruments inside huge glass cabinets along the walls. The rich smell of sycamore and maple wood highly varnished, the beauty of the craftsmanship on the carvings of the violin scrolls, the splendour of really expensive bows . . . all this was a thrill to Elizabeth. Some of the bows were mounted in gold, some in silver with mother-of-pearl insets; others looked splendid in ebony, ivory and tortoiseshell.

Gio played excerpts from his favourite solos and then a sequence from the Elgar Concerto, producing a golden tone which, to Elizabeth, seemed quite out of this world. After thoroughly trying out each instrument, checking on the harmonies and the double-stopping, he laid them in a row across the table in order of merit: the Amati, the Guarnarius, three Stradivarius, two Guadagnini, and four Joseph Roccas. It was a difficult choice for the boy but, in the end, he did come to a decision.

A warm feeling had overtaken Elizabeth's heart as she watched the cherub-like face registering such obvious delight. She had noted the entranced expression with which he played, his eyes closed for long periods, and when he looked up in between snatches of melody, that overwhelming trust shone once more from his eyes.

His voice was eager now: 'This is the one I prefer, Elizabeth! Not so much the artistry of the carvings, but the feel of it as I play. It seems to be part of me. I play on this fiddle as if I am possessed by it . . . as if it is part of my very soul!'

So Elizabeth brought out her cheque book and settled the account for twelve thousand pounds, signing the cheque with a flourish and a clear conscience. The violin was placed in its velvet-lined case of brown leather, and handed over to the boy. It was an authentic Guarnarius dated 1820, highly polished in a warm russet hue, the four black pegs holding the strings inlaid with gold.

They crossed the city again by taxi and Elizabeth walked tall and felt proud as they entered the train and took seats in an empty compartment. Both had a feeling of jubilation on the homeward journey. Giovanni covered her hand with his and at that moment they had never been closer.

She continued to feel totally justified. This young man was entitled to the finest quality of life during the time that remained to him. If Roger did not agree it would be just too bad. Later, on, she would emphasise, the violin could be resold and the money repaid into the bank. But she must not allow such morbid thoughts to take root in her mind.

That evening, in the privacy of her lounge, Elizabeth watched Giovanni playing on his new instrument. She noted the ethereal look on his face and a glow of warm satisfaction seeped through her sorrow: she had, beyond the shadow of a doubt, done the right thing.

Chapter 10

Elizabeth racked her brains to think of some way of dealing with Idris and his followers. Far better to keep the whole thing peaceful and sensible: she was not in the habit of returning evil for evil. Yet, with the memory of Peter's damaged car and that dreadful commotion at the pier head cafe fresh in her mind, it was difficult to think in a clear detached way.

On an impulse, one Monday morning, she stuffed a jar of gooseberry jam into her bag together with a pile of out-of-date magazines and set off for the smallholding. On Mondays, Zechariah and Idris sold pigs in Abergele market, away from the house for at least four hours. More satisfactory to deal with the matter woman to woman, Elizabeth had decided, and she wished to avoid any confrontation with Zechariah or Idris.

According to a brief item in the *Chronicle*, Idris had been suspended from Council meetings for the time being, in view of certain unseemly behaviour not in keeping with town council constitution. That would still be a sore point with the family, and Elizabeth had no idea what kind of a reception she was in for. With a deep breath, she left her car in the lane and went to open the rickety gate of the smallholding.

The drive was overgrown with long grass, nettles and weeds. Several discarded implements were strewn about and a pile of scattered glass lay below a broken window in one of the out-buildings.

A sheep dog barked and fussed about round her legs and a gaggle of noisy geese almost frightened the life out of her as she approached the shabby front door. Smoke came out of a nearby chimney and there was a strong smell of pig food on the boil. This, mingled with the odour of cow manure and stale hen-food, was enough to turn Elizabeth's stomach over. She gritted her teeth, put her best foot forward, and, offering up a silent prayer, gave three short taps on the door.

It was the first time she had come face to face with Gwyneth. There was a certain tiredness about the woman's long pale features, a jaded look in the dark brown eyes. Broad and strong, with thin, lank brown hair across her forehead, she looked neglected. A coarse apron covered her faded skirt, which came down well below the tops of her black wellingtons. As she opened the door and peered out, Elizabeth volunteered in a cheery tone:

'Good morning, Mrs. Jones. My apologies for bothering you at this time of day, but I wondered if you could very kindly spare me two dozen eggs? I prefer free-range ones for my visitors and yours, I've heard, are particularly large.'

Gwyneth was evidently not deluded: 'If it's about Idris you have come, Mrs. Williams, I have nothing to say. What would you be here for but to talk about my son?' She spoke in a monotone which reminded Elizabeth of the drone of a vacuum cleaner.

With a distinct feeling the door was about to be slammed in her face, she forced a smile and a nervous laugh as she took Gwyneth's hand in hers:

'Don't get me wrong, Mrs. Jones. I haven't come here to make trouble: life's too short for that isn't it? Your son has some very good points.'

At this Gwyneth melted visibly, a look of definite pride appearing on plain features.

'A good boy he is Mrs. Williams, and our only son.'

'Of course he is.' Elizabeth swallowed and then continued, 'Doesn't every mother think that about her own son? You must have great hopes for Idris, ambitions and such like.'

Gwyneth avoided her eyes then, looking down at her feet.

'His father it is. He wants him to make a big name for himself and be famous. I don't go along with it, mind.'

'There's no reason why he shouldn't be famous, Mrs. Jones — or may I call you Gwyneth? He has such confidence: a boy who could go far if only he gets the right advice from his parents.'

Gwyneth, considering this thoughtfully, seemed rather at a loss for words.

'You know, Gwyneth,' Elizabeth continued, choosing her words with care, 'there'll always be a gulf between people where music is concerned; no real solution to that problem. Your son is gifted in one kind of music and the people I mix with are gifted in another type altogether. I know how broad minded you are, having travelled abroad and met people of all tastes and cultures. Don't you agree, we should be able to give and take? Everybody must give a little, We can't all take.'

With Gwyneth clearly taking all this in, she went on after a pause:

'By all means let Idris have his group — in the Community Centre or the Town Hall, I would suggest — and there's no reason why the two types of music should not carry on. This is an attractive town and people flock to this area, coming hundreds of miles to admire our scenery. Elderly folk, in particular, enjoy the pier concerts. Surely we can drown our differences and come to terms with the problem? You will help, won't you?'

'I see what you mean. I never thought of it like that.' Gwyneth opened the door wider and stepped back into the hall: 'Would you like to come inside, Mrs. Williams? Silly it is standing here on the step.'

'Thanks. Oh, by the way, I've brought you this jar of home-made jam and these woman's magazines . . .'

Elizabeth entered the house somewhat boldly, not knowing what to expect. She caught sight, through an open doorway, of what seemed like the whole of Idris's drum kit. She counted five drums in assorted sizes, all chromium plated and gleaming brightly in contrast to shabby furniture. There was a large electronic organ padded out in a bright green plastic material with what seemed like thousands of stops above the keyboard in various colours. Two electric guitars stood in one corner and the microphone and amplifying equipment filled one whole wall. This elaborate set-up must have cost a fortune, Elizabeth mused, and his mother must have felt as proud as a peacock each time he set off in his brightly coloured gear.

Idris had become more of a problem, Gwyneth confided, ever since he had got mixed up with this group. He had always been a loner, moody and difficult, but lately he had been drinking too much and she would like to see him settling down with a nice local girl and living a normal life.

Her husband made all the decisions in their house, she went on, she never having a say in anything. If she had her way, she'd

80

have been doing bed and breakfast in a nice tidy farm, with her own money to spend.

As Elizabeth watched the woman washing the eggs in the low stone sink in the old-fashioned kitchen, she felt nothing but pity. How sad that Gwyneth should spend her life in such surroundings, dominated by an unreasonable husband and putting up with the tantrums of an over-indulged son!

Gwyneth promised to have a talk with both husband and son and try to get them to see reason.

'Only it's not me as decides things . . .' Her hand half covered her mouth in case she should be overheard. 'It's Zech as tells us what to do. I fall in line to keep the peace, just as I've done all these years.'

Elizabeth came away with mixed feelings. If she hadn't made a friend, at least she had not created an enemy. And now she could but live in hope.

* * * *

'You must be out of your mind, Liz! You've actually bought this posh violin — for a boy you hardly know?'

Naomi sounded both amazed and censorious, and Elizabeth was glad they were the only customers in that corner of the cafe. It was intended to be a quick coffee after a spot of shopping together.

'What of it?' She deliberately tried to sound casual, as if it was a perfectly natural thing to do. 'I gave it to him for a present, that's all.'

'But darling, what a risk! The boy could disappear back where he came from and sell it. Where will you be then?'

Elizabeth sipped her coffee and helped herself to a buttered scone. It would be prudent to change the subject: she was quite out of her depth. But Naomi hadn't finished, seemingly brimful of her usual wordly wisdom.

'I bet he's not paying for his keep, either. Am I right?'

'I don't charge him anything. But it's too late to talk like that now, Naomi. Don't you realise he won't be here much longer?'

'If you ask me, he ought to go back to that Home,' Naomi insisted. 'There must be a Care Order on him and it may not have expired. You really shouldn't burden yourself with an invalid in a busy house like yours.'

'I couldn't do that.' Elizabeth's voice trembled with suppressed annoyance. 'I'm not like that . . .'

'I'll tell you something else,' her friend interrupted. 'I'm only trying to help, darling, and it's for your own good. Someone I know used to foster children. They never appreciate anything you do for them, she told me. They go about all their life with a kingsized chip on their shoulder, as if the world owes them something. Giovanni won't thank you for any of this.'

Elizabeth felt hurt that Naomi of all people, whose opinion she had always valued, should talk to her so. Well, she had heard enough! Politely but firmly she got up to go, paid at the cash desk and made for her car. Then, with a few brief words of farewell, she drove home.

She did not often feel annoyed but this kind of advice, quite unsolicited, made her blood boil. She had intended to keep secret the fact that she had paid for the expensive violin, but, as orchestral members had been visiting Gio at the house, and as the violin looked and sounded so superior to any other violin for miles around, the news had inevitably leaked out. Several people had told her she was mad, and a few had volunteered that Gio should go back to Manchester. One well meaning 'friend' had actually had the audacity to remark that she should consider the welfare of her guests. After all leukaemia was cancer, she had insisted, and therefore contagious and a menace to society. How *could* people be so inhuman? They obviously thought she regarded Gio as just another lodger with a bed to be changed and a mouth to feed. They could not know that, in her heart of hearts, she looked upon him as her long-lost son.

*   *   *   *

'You've come after all, Elizabeth! We didn't think you'd make it.'

Helen was doing her best to close the zip of a bulging shoulder bag, stuffing her red plastic mac further in to make room for a white cardigan and a pair of sun glasses.

'I didn't expect to make it either,' Elizabeth replied. 'But as soon as I heard for sure that Mr. Simpson, Giovanni's favourite tutor, was coming for the day, and that Gretta was prepared to stay in and cook for them, I just knew I was intended to come on the outing after all.'

It was the day of the Palm Court Orchestra's annual trip. All the musicians and most of the friends of the orchestra had turned up, casually dressed in bright coloured anoracs with cameras and binoculars swinging from their shoulders. The red and white coach looked clean and comfortable as fifty or so passengers trooped in, swooping down on the best window seats and throwing coats and bags onto the luggage racks. The driver, smart in cream linen jacket and red peak cap, was helping the older ones carefully up the steep coach steps.

Bill, one of the 'friends', armed with clipboard and biro, ticked off the names as each one entered, and there was plenty of laughter and excited chatter.

'There we are, folks, that's the lot,' announced Bill. 'I make it fifty-two. Don't worry about the rain, due to stop within the hour. See that big patch of blue over the sea? We're in for a fine day.'

His voice was cheerful and optimistic.

'Hope you've all got your packed lunches. We'll be eating in the grounds of Plas Newydd at Llangollen. But our first stop, ladies and gentlemen, is for coffee at Betws-y-coed.'

Much hard work had gone into organising this trip, usually one of the highlights of the season. The 'friends' had paid an advance visit to ensure that the stately home Plas Newydd expected them, and that the hotel at the foot of the Horseshoe Pass was up to standard for their afternoon tea. The trip on the canal had been sampled and the suitability of the various exhibitions and museums checked.

Immensely though she enjoyed these outings, Elizabeth had been reluctant to put her name down this year. How could she leave Gio? He had his good days but, she knew, would never stand the strain of a whole day out in such a crowd. Then, like a ray of sunshine on a dull day, this letter had arrived. Mr. Simpson, the tutor he had talked so much about when he first came, had suggested visiting Swallow Tree Gardens for a whole day to find out for himself just how his former pupil was. Elizabeth had felt then that she could leave with an easy mind, having given Gretta full instructions to ensure that all three would have a good nourishing lunch.

At the same time, it proved a difficult choice, torn as she felt between two loyalties. Should she stay behind to enjoy intellectual conversation with Mr. Simpson and witness Gio's reaction to

83

seeing his former tutor? She would have relished that. But she was also drawn to the prospect of spending a whole day in the company of her beloved orchestra. In particular she would enjoy a chat with Peter about some of the things so dear to her heart. She would tell him of the slight possibility, mentioned by her doctor, that Giovanni's life could be prolonged by a series of blood transfusions. Vague and indefinite though the idea was, it did at least offer a glimmer of hope. Elizabeth felt like a swimmer clutching at straws. Anything, just anything, must be tried that came along!

The day was a continuous round of jollity and high spirits, with Peter Emmanual showing even more vitality than usual. Elizabeth caught sight of him shaking with merriment and showing all his teeth as Clive told him the funniest joke imaginable. She hadn't realised before that a musical director could be so full of humour, so adaptable to the enthusiasm of his surroundings.

Everybody brought out their sandwiches as tables and chairs were arranged on the huge lawn overlooking Plas Newydd. The super-abundance of hydrangeas in brilliant shades of blue and mauve made an excellent setting for the picnic. Elizabeth noticed that Sylvia had brought a big polythene food box full of delicious savouries for herself and Martin. Blue eyes dancing, she gazed up at him, laughing at his jokes with more gusto than they deserved.

As the party trooped single file around the historic house, Elizabeth particularly admired the artistry in the cedarwood and mahogany furniture, the ebony carvings adorning the mantelpieces, and the collection of musical instruments, Welsh harp, spinet and harpsichord, which must have been handed down several generations of Lady Eleanor and Lady Sarah's family.

Elizabeth was lulled into a delicious feeling of contentment as the whole party took a sixty minute trip down the famous canal on the gondola-type barge, meandering between fields of luscious pastures where cattle grazed and weeping willows hung over the water. As the barge moved by, families of fluffy ducklings moved swiftly away into their nests in the grass verges. The youth in charge steered the white cart horse, attached by a thick rope to the barge, and walking at a leisurely pace along the canal bank. Patrick had brought his guitar and, as he strummed away in a far corner, everybody joined in with his popular folk music and

84

dreamy love songs. All this gave Elizabeth a wonderful feeling of rapture.

The Welsh Dragon Hotel, overlooking the Horeshoe Pass, put on an excellent tea, the menu being written in Welsh and the waitresses dressed in traditional Welsh costume, white aprons over long red dresses and tall black hats. As everyone tucked into turkey salad, helping themselves to luscious sauces and trimmings, Elizabeth was first to notice Sylvia waving her left hand about to draw attention to her cluster-of-diamond engagement ring.

'We saw it in a jeweller's window in Llangollen,' she announced. 'Martin just led me into the shop and it fitted perfectly. So now we're engaged.'

Elizabeth felt as happy as if it were her own daughter. What an unbelievable change had come over the timid girl of only a few weeks ago!

Congratulations were heaped upon the couple and Elizabeth was especially pleased to hear that Martin had already taught Sylvia how to play the viola. They regularly played duets together, she gathered, and Sylvia was competent to sight-read and play any of the orchestral pieces without difficulty. It was also noticeable that the unsociable Richard had not mixed very well on the outing, but had remained on the fringe of everything, with rather a blank look on his face, the whole of the day.

The journey home turned out to be a real scream, each musician vying with his colleagues to tell the wittiest true story. Peter told of an occasion when his baton had flown out of his hand during a particularly lively passage in a Haydn Symphony, hitting the bass player and knocking off his spectacles. The startled player had leaned forward to retrieve them, only to knock over a couple of music stands, with the result that pages and pages of music had flown over the stage, much to the amusement of the audience.

Les recounted the time when, during a power failure, complete darkness had descended on the stage in the middle of a Tchaikovsky Symphony. The musicians had continued playing, some from memory, others just busking along, and even the conductor had continued, beating time to an invisible orchestra. He knew the show must go on, Les remarked laughingly, and within ten minutes the lights had flickered on again and all was back to normal.

Patrick, first violin, told of an occasion when he had stood up before an audience all ready to play for his solo Bach's *Air on the G String*. Suddenly his G string had broken and flown into his face. He had panicked for a second and, instead of apologising and going back stage to borrow another fiddle, he had played the work right through an octave higher, using the D and A strings. The total effect had been lost, of course, but the audience had clapped like mad. This story brought roars of laughter throughout the coach, Elizabeth feeling her sides aching as she chuckled away. Never in all her life had she laughed so much.

It was almost half past six and the coach, approaching the town, pulled up at a set of traffic lights near to 'The Mountain View'. Elizabeth noticed a bunch of young men coming out of the bar in high spirits. There was a crowd of passers-by on the pavement so it was impossible to see exactly what happened.

Suddenly, hearing a shattering of glass, she looked towards the back of the coach. A big hole could be seen in the window and a jagged stone hurtling between the passengers' faces. Missing Peter's eyes by a hair's breadth, the missile landed in Martin's lap as he and Sylvia sat holding hands.

Everybody sprang up, some of the women starting to scream. Martin produced a handkerchief and mopped up the blood spilling over Sylvia's white dress. The back of his hand was oozing with blood and there was a nasty gash across his wrist.

A woman on the pavement ran up to stand on the steps of the coach and shout to the driver:

'I saw that. Saw it with my own eyes, I did! The culprit is that chap running away like mad. See him? The one in the red jacket and green trousers.'

Another woman joined her. 'I know the one who did it,' she announced. 'It was Idris Jones — that pig farmer's son who plays the drums and dresses all posh!'

Elizabeth's heart felt as heavy as lead. What an end to a delightful day . . . She gazed at poor Martin as he bound several layers of handkerchief around his wrist, holding his arm awkwardly as if in pain.

So Idris Jones was up to his tricks again: so much for her attempts at reconciliation! I suppose we are now back to square one, she told herself. And where do we go from here?

Chapter 11

Elizabeth found it strange indeed to be sitting in the audience with Martin by her side, his hand bandaged, his arm slung up round his neck. The doctor at the surgery had insisted on an anti-tetanus injection and warned that it would be at least a week before his fingers would be nimble enough to play in the orchestra.

With only two hours to go before the concert, Peter was still desperately trying to find a substitute. Waving the familiar musicians' year book, he complained bitterly about the near non-existence of viola players in North Wales. There was page upon page of violinists but only two names for the viola, one in Bangor, the other in Wrexham.

Finally, doing her best to be helpful, Elizabeth suggested, 'Why not try Sylvia?'

'She is so young — and has had no experience!' Peter sounded at his wits' end. 'Whatever *are* we going to do?'

It was Martin who convinced him that Sylvia could cope:

'She's not the same girl you took on, Peter, and I've taught her the very pieces scheduled for tonight. We've played them together several times. You'd be surprised how her confidence has increased . . .'

'I'm sure I can do it,' beamed Sylvia. 'Honestly, I'll be O.K. on my own! After all Martin has drummed into me, how could I be otherwise?'

This was indeed the happiest day of her life, she felt — the day Martin had bought her this fabulous ring. True, it could have been spoiled by his hand injury and the bloodstain on her new white dress. Yet still she felt like a fairy tale princess and as if she were walking in the clouds. On top of all this happiness, she

87

was about to leave stuffy old Richard with the second-fiddle image he bore, and join the ranks of the lower strings, over in the bass section where the music always sounded so beautiful and mellow.

The concert started well and Sylvia never took her eyes off the music except to watch, with half an eye, the beat of that white baton in Peter Emmanual's right hand. She was totally unaware of Martin and Elizabeth watching her a few feet away on the other side of the footlights and potted plants.

The interval came in what seemed no time at all and she skipped along to the cafe.

'Oh, it was wonderful,' she enthused, eyes dancing as she joined Martin and Elizabeth for coffee. 'I seemed to be transported into another world. You're right, Martin, the viola *is* a more satisfying instrument than strumming away at second violin.'

'I'm delighted it came off so well.' He held her hand tightly, gazing adoringly into her upturned face. 'Peter is equally delighted, you may be sure.'

Taking the good with the bad, Elizabeth decided, the day had not been too disappointing after all. The following evening, however, her strength and vitality seemed to have disappeared and she felt the day had been one of complete frustration.

Peter was on the phone at almost seven o'clock, checking up that she would attend the concert for sure.

'It's quite impossible, Peter. I simply can't make it: I've never felt so exhausted.'

'That doesn't sound like you, my dear.' His disappointment was obvious. 'You've hardly missed a concert this season.'

'Well, that's how it is. Blame Vic Simpson, will you?'

'Oh yes, I meant to warn you about him. Not really to be trusted, you know. Only after the shekels. He takes on the brilliant students, the ones that will make him famous, and leaves all others alone.'

'I do wish you had warned me. Well, it's too late now.'

Why did she always do things on impulse? Elizabeth's heart sank like a stone thrown into water. In this case it would have been wiser to ask Peter's advice.

'I phoned because I thought you might have helped me out with entertaining the Weissmans — you know, sitting by them and chatting them up. We owe them some hospitality after their generous gift to our funds. You remember them, of course?' Peter continued in a self-satisfied tone. 'They judged our talent contest last season and Dr. Weissman gave a quite unforgettable resumé at the end.'

Elizabeth didn't remember at all. How could she keep in mind all the fans of Peter Emmanual who attended year after year to hear his music? This kind of thing tended to make him more conceited than ever. But she had just arrived home from a most tedious day in Manchester and it was out of the question for her to attend the concert. Peter had to be told.

This Vic Simpson, she pondered as she returned to the kitchen, had not turned out a bit like the tutor she had imagined. Young, with smart city clothes and a glossy well-shaped hair style, he was a fluent talker, but a poor listener, his big brown eyes flitting about all over the room. Also he had a habit of moving jerkily from one foot to the other in a restless way. True enough, he had been Gio's favourite tutor, but that was two years ago. And now Peter had warned her that he was out only to make money on his brilliant pupils and bask in the reflected glory they gave him!

Vic Simpson had cleverly talked Elizabeth into taking Gio that same day to see his old Master and Matron at the children's home. 'He'll love that, Mrs. Williams,' he had enthused, 'and it's the least we can do for him while he's well enough to travel.'

But that had not been the end of it. Once in Manchester, this persistent young man had hoodwinked her into agreeing to have studio photographs taken of Gio with his new violin. Naturally enough the boy had gone along with the idea. This had snow-balled into a long session at the recording studio, with Vic rushing around giving orders to everybody in sight. A small grand piano had stood in the middle of a huge array of recording equipment and Vic had sat down and accompanied Gio while he played enough solos to cover sixty minutes of tape. They had waited in a side-room while these were transferred on to long playing records, Vic keeping up a one-sided conversation about it being essential to have it all down for the sake of the record, and the photographs and recordings published and preserved for the sake of posterity.

Elizabeth was not impressed. What was the point of tiring the boy out, tearing him across the city from one place to another with scarcely a minute in which to eat or even breathe? She was relieved when they had finally stepped out of Vic's white

Bentley and retrieved the violin from the back seat where, covered over with a travelling rug, it had survived the hectic journey.

There had scarcely been time to give Vic a proper send off. Before she realised it, he was gone. Her anxiety increased when she learned from Gretta that the previous day, when she had been on the trip, Vic Simpson had done nothing but ask questions and write down all the information he had gained in a large exercise book.

'What sort of questions, Gretta? Surely he knew all he needed to know: I went into details with him about Gio's condition.' Such a lack of etiquette on the part of an educated man frankly amazed Elizabeth.

'Oh, thousands of questions!' Gretta waved her arms about, her tone pitched higher as she tried to make her point. 'What did I think of 'im? Did I 'ave any, what do you say, rapport, or relationship with 'im? What does 'e 'ave for breakfast? Oh, Mrs. Williams, 'e 'ad me all confused! Real mad I was. And you know something? 'E seems to be writing a book.'

Then the penny dropped. This Vic was anxious to be first in the field when it came to Gio's end. He intended to dramatise his short life, commercialise it, bring out all his photographs and information and make a small fortune.

So furious was Elizabeth, at that instant, that she resolved to phone Peter, tell him all she knew, and see what, if anything, he could do to prohibit Vic's hateful scheme.

*   *   *   *

Elizabeth had almost forgotten that it was the day for Roger to come home permanently. She was as excited as he when, like a ten year old arriving home from boarding school, he threw his suitcase into his room and started looking around for any changes in the house. Rushing up to him, she put both arms round his neck and held him tight, relief surging like red wine through her veins.

'Oh Roger, it's grand to have you home at last! It is true, isn't it? You *are* home for good?

It was long since she had given him so affectionate a welcome, thrilled as she was to see him standing there.

'Quite true, my sweet one,' he chuckled. 'Four weeks holiday and then we start up this factory installation at Wrexham in September. Get the kettle on, and then you can tell me all about young Gio. I was really upset to receive your letter. Surely they haven't given him up completely?'

Roger's case was now opened up across the bed and he was sorting through assorted clothing to find a small square parcel. Grinning, he handed it to Elizabeth.

'My favourite perfume,' she murmured, more thrilled by the kind thought than by the actual gift. As she sprayed a sample over his pullover, its fragrance filled the room.

'I fear the news is no better, Roger.' She handed him a cup of tea and a buttered scone. 'The hospital's verdict remains as I told you in the letter . . .at most he has only six to twelve months . . .' The last word ended in a stifled sob.

Elizabeth felt oh so comforted when Roger put a tender arm around her and smiled his most sympathetic smile.

'The blood transfusions didn't work out,' she continued. 'My doctor thought they might do a bit of good, but Gio's case appears to be more acute. It seems hopeless, Roger, with no light at all at the end of the tunnel.'

'How difficult it must be for you to keep up an appearance of cheerfulness when he's around.' Roger's soothing voice was like velvet to her ears, the kind of therapy she needed.

'Tell you what, why don't I take him fishing? I'll get a boat and we'll go out together all round Anglesey. That should put colour into his cheeks and give him an appetite for one of your gorgeous meals. It's right what you said in your letter: we must give Gio as full a life as possible. You can rely on me for that just now, with all this time on my hands.'

Roger, of all people, taking an interest in the boy, Elizabeth marvelled. How satisfying to think she would now have him around to advise her. Peter had such a one-track mind, far too occupied with his concerts to give proper thought to Gio's illness. He might have taken on the legal guardianship in a temporary capacity, but he left the decisions to her, never interfering in any way; with his implicit trust in her it suited him to leave everything to her. In future, she decided, she would listen more to Roger. As a man of the world, he would have useful advice to offer and they would now have far more time to talk things over together.

The matron at the children's home had sounded very possessive over the phone. They wanted Giovanni back where he belonged: they had reared him and knew more about him than anyone. She made it clear to Elizabeth that she intended to put in a claim.

It's like being in a maze, she thought. Here I am surrounded by hedges six feet tall, with all these paths looking exactly alike, and only one of them leading out into the light. If only I could put the clock back three months! Then life was perfect: I floated on a cloud of ecstasy, completely carried away. How it's all come crashing down on me like so much debris after a raid.

The maze was made even more complicated when Peter arrived at Swallow Tree Gardens at almost eleven o'clock, accompanied by Dr. Weissman. Her brows shot up as she saw the two men standing there at such an hour.

'Hallo, Elizabeth. You missed a good concert tonight. We had a full house too: they simply wouldn't let us go.'

How like Peter to praise his own concerts! He never got any better, she reflected, he was just full of himself.

'May I introduce Dr. Eberhart Weissman, my dear? He has come all the way from Geneva.' Turning to his friend, Peter continued with enthusiasm: 'This is my good friend Elizabeth Williams, a tower of strength to me and one of our chief supporters at the concerts.'

By the time they were all seated in her lounge, enjoying a glass of sherry, Elizabeth had noticed a sheaf of papers in Dr. Weissman's hands, together with a coloured brochure and a business-like file.

'Elizabeth,' Peter broke the silence after taking a gulp of sherry, 'let us get straight to the point. Dr. Weissman is very interested in Giovanni's case. He has his own clinic on the banks of Lake Geneva, and he has suggested to me, as Gio's guardian, that he should take the boy back with him at the end of the week.'

Dr. Eberhart Weissman was a tall, erect man in his early sixties, with thick waves of shining white hair. His skin was healthy and tanned and his clear blue eyes were unusually penetrating. As well as an educated accent, with a slight German intonation, he possessed an old-world charm rarely found these days, and his handshake, firm and confident, displayed strength of personality. His well-cut suit showed elegance and good taste and he had an excellent command of the English language.

Elizabeth felt a stab of anxiety and resentment at the mere

thought of Gio being taken away from her. Why did her maternal instinct work overtime every time this kind of situation arose? For the sake of politeness, however, she must not dismiss the idea without hearing the full story.

'But — what can you possibly do for him, Dr. Weissman?' she exclaimed. 'It is accepted the case we are dealing with is terminal. Giovanni himself is prepared to accept the inevitable. So what point would there be in taking him from what he has come to regard as his home?'

'A good question, madam.' Dr. Weissman's manner was undoubtedly persuasive. 'I have at my clinic equipment for tests. I do experiments, Frau Williams, and find out things that no one else finds. Thus I would welcome this case for observation purposes, and for the sake of other patients with that complaint. You see?'

Elizabeth had heard enough. Her mind went blank as this man tried to explain to her what he had in mind. Seeing the look of disgust on her face, it was Peter who intervened:

'No harm done, Liz. We will go now and leave you to think about it. When you've mentioned it to Gio, let me know what he decides. The decision should, after all, be his.'

That night in bed, Elizabeth felt the maze getting darker and thicker. It seemed impossible to find a way out into the sunlight. How dare anyone suggest making experiments on a person already content to spend his few remaining months in peace and security? Only yesterday Gio had confided that Swallow Tree Gardens was the place where he wanted to be when the end came: the place where he had found perfect peace. He wished for nothing more than to relax in the grounds, watching the cows and listening to the birds.

The very word 'experiment' suggested torture. Thoughts of vivisection haunted Elizabeth most of the night, her mind filled with horror at the idea of allowing Gio to go off to what she considered must be a place of torment and barbarity.

It was quite dark, but a quarter moon could be seen, sharply outlined against the blackness of the sky. The house was perfectly still and quiet and the illuminated clock on her bedside table registered three o'clock.

She put out a hand beneath the blankets and, for the first time in many years, she felt the warmth of her man, the strong reliable Roger, lying fast asleep beside her.

A pleasant feeling of consolation and comfort overtook her and, with a sigh of relief, as if a certain weight had been taken off her mind, she drifted into a peaceful sleep.

Chapter 12

'You definitely over-reacted, Liz. As soon as Dr. Weissman mentioned taking Gio away you didn't listen any more now, did you?'

Roger was studying the brochure which had been left in the lounge the previous evening, a pictorial guide, in four languages, displaying a colourful picture of the lakes and mountains of Switzerland. As he turned over the pages between mouthfuls of bacon and sips of coffee, his eye caught one of the paragraphs and he looked up with interest.

'I say, according to these photos it's a mansion of a place — and just look at this plan of the clinic! There's a surgery for physiotherapy and X-ray with an annexe here for electronic blood tests. They have their own psychiatrist — and a brain scanner and a psychotherapy unit. There's two long wards there, with sixty beds in each, a lecture room, and a big section in that annexe for acupuncture.'

Roger looked quite excited as he turned over another page.

'This Weissman fella seems to be a disciple of Harry Benjamen. Remember all that talk about nature cures when we were kids? The patients at this clinic get 100% whole raw food, everything compost grown and nothing refined.'

Rather nonplussed, Elizabeth wished she could recall some hint in last night's conversation about the possibility of a cure.

'Sounds all right to me, luv,' Roger was saying. 'How about having another talk with the chap? I'll arrange to be there, and Gio too, so that he can decide. I don't suppose the poor lad has even heard about it yet.'

'Well, if you really think so, Roger,' she replied doubtfully. 'I suppose I was too emotional last night. I gave the man no chance to explain properly. It was rather late when they arrived and, as I told you, I was over-tired to start with.'

Elizabeth's mind was turning over like so much gravel in a concrete mixer. Still indignant about Vic Simpson's commercial approach to Gio's illness, and exasperated with all the unwanted advice being heaped upon her, she found it difficult to think in her customary logical way.

What exactly was Dr. Weissman getting at? She did recall a vague mention of acupuncture and the very word had sent cold shivers rushing down her spine. Did this man merely wish to make experiments, or did he hope for a cure? Foolish to turn it down, of course, if there were the remotest chance of a recovery. But would Gio agree to going all that way and giving up his composition and violin playing? It was amazing how calm and serene the boy was, never showing any self-pity or depression; his oval face full of determination as he pored over his manuscript book. He seemed to display an inner courage and had absolutely no fear of death.

One evening he had burst in, book and pencil in hand: 'Most of the composers died young, Elizabeth, and Schubert in particular — but look how their works live on! They all had something to work for. Yes, their lives had purpose . . . And so has mine. I intend to get these manuscripts into the hands of Dr. Emmanual very soon now, and I shan't be happy till they arrive at the printers.'

She had not got round to telling Roger about the expensive violin. She would have to work on that one. She should, she knew, have confided in him straight away, but a twinge of conscience had made her hesitate. Now, with so much else to be thought about and decided, the question of the Guarnarius violin would have to wait.

Roger, still turning the pages of the glossy brochure, read out slowly and deliberately:

' 'We serve nothing but whole foods, rich in minerals and natural salts, and all our medication is purely herbal.' They have a section for Yoga and relaxation, Liz — Swedish massage Scottish Douch, and Seaweed Therapy. And they even mention faith healing and transcendental meditation. 'It is when the medical profession gives up that we step in. Our methods are as near to nature as possible . . .' Well, they've certainly got the lot! Heaven only knows what all this must cost. You'd indeed have to be wealthy to stay at such a place. So why should this doctor be so keen on getting the boy in there — just a homeless kid as far as he is concerned?'

'It's all covered, Roger, — run by some benevolent fund where you only pay what you can afford. In Gio's case, because he was in care for so long, Dr. Weissman said it would be free.'

Gio appeared. He was usually so solemn and quiet that she was surprised to see his face lit up with joy at the prospect of the day's fishing with Roger.

Taking his place at table, he picked up the brochure. 'Is someone going abroad? I like the look of that blue lake and those snow-capped mountains.' He started reading the text. As Elizabeth poured out his tea, her eyes met Roger's and then they both studied Gio's face. At length he broke the silence:

'So that's it, you want me to go to this place! I sensed something in the air, and when that chap came with Peter last night I sort of got the message.'

'It's only an idea, Gio. A suggestion of Peter's.' Elizabeth deliberately made her voice sound calm and controlled. 'Dr. Weissman isn't a doctor of music, as we first thought, but a doctor of medicine. And the idea of this clinic is something we shall have to think out very carefully. Have a good look at it. You, after all, are the one who will have to decide whether to go in for it or not.'

Gio turned back the pages of the brochure and started reading from the beginning. Meanwhile Elizabeth disappeared into the kitchen to rescue a saucepan of milk, which she started pouring into a flask. Never before had her hand felt so unsteady, her mind so disturbed or her tummy so wobbly.

With his quick brain Giovanni absorbed the contents of the guide in a matter of minutes. As he turned to the last page his face was radiant:

'I say, you two, this chap's a religious man. He has his own chapel and it says here what a large part prayer and faith play in his treatment. He quotes from the book of James in the New Testament: 'The prayer of faith shall save the sick'. And further down: 'Whatsoever ye shall ask in my name, believing, ye shall receive.' I'm sure he's got something there.'

Gio spoke almost as if he had received some private message. 'The strange thing, Elizabeth, is that this must be an answer to prayer.' So full of earnestness his voice sounded, so full of reverence, that Elizabeth looked astonished at Roger.

'You know how placidly I've accepted this illness,' Giovanni continued in a low, confiding tone. 'Well, I'm not afraid to die. But I did pray for help and courage to endure what was coming to me and also for a way out, if there was one. Matron started me off, you know. She got me going on private prayer, besides our assemblies in the hall every morning. And she also suggested I read a chapter of the Bible every day. You've no idea how that can help at such a time as this.'

Elizabeth felt a pang of guilt. Her mind had been so preoccupied that she'd hardly remembered her Christian upbringing. And now here was this boy reminding her. Clearly it was the religious aspect of this scheme which appealed to Gio, whereas the 'whole foods' idea had caught Roger's imagination. She couldn't help wondering why Dr. Weissman hadn't mentioned religion when he called. Roger pointed out that he couldn't have told her everything in one short talk and, anyway, she had hardly been receptive at the time.

Finishing his coffee, Roger got up from the table as he added half jokingly: 'That man's just about covered everything. If one thing fails there's something else to try . . . Well, Gio, shall we be off? Plenty of time to discuss this later.'

With an affectionate kiss for Elizabeth, he picked up the lunch basket and fishing tackle, about to make for the garage. Gio hesitated as if deep in thought, and then, passing through the doorway after Roger, he flashed back:

'You read it, Elizabeth, while we're out. It might be providence that sent that man here.'

'Mind you don't get cold sitting about,' she shouted after them. 'And be sure to take your tablets, Gio.'

With that they were off.

Even more Elizabeth felt she had not yet plumbed the depths of this strange boy. There were surprises all the way. Another interview would have to be arranged with this unusual doctor, and she must bring herself to think positively and optimistically about the Swiss health clinic.

If only she wasn't lumbered with so many visitors, she could have left everything and gone with him! But there was nobody she could trust to take over Swallow Tree Gardens, and her booking chart showed another four weeks to see the season

98

through. As she waved goodbye to the two men she felt that at least part of the burden had been lifted from her shoulders and there was a glimmer of light at the end of the tunnel.

But she must concentrate on breakfasts. In the event she had to cope on her own. Gretta appeared at the kitchen door, looking as white as a sheet and saying she felt too groggy to serve breakfast. So Elizabeth had the joint role of cook and waitress. She must get those breakfasts on to the table by nine. Come to think of it, Gretta had been quite lethargic these last few days. Was she missing her family or, perhaps, hankering after her homeland? Her usual verve was missing and she was far from the cheerful girl she had been. Elizabeth only hoped it was nothing serious as she started to lay the tables.

*   *   *   *

'Hello, Elizabeth! Sylvia's just gone in through the stage door, so I thought I'd come and sit by you again.'

Martin looked cool in a cream open neck shirt as he took his seat beside Elizabeth for the third time that week. There was less and less bandage on his injured wrist each night. The swelling had gone down, she noticed, and the bruising almost disappeared.

'Yes, Martin, these seats are as good as any,' she rejoined. 'I say, isn't Sylvia doing well? Such a transformation: I never saw a girl look so sure of herself or, at the same time, so radiant. But what's happened to the audience tonight?' she added, turning to survey empty rows. 'There's hardly anybody here.'

'Only regulars tonight,' Martin confirmed. 'There's a counter attraction, a military band, at the bandstand. We'll probably hear it coming across the water on a calm night like this. Nothing like a military band to draw the crowds.'

'Oh yes, I remember now. And wasn't there something in the *Chronicle* about a shortage of trombone players, and they also wanted another bassoon?'

'That's right. They've put on a talent contest as well. The visitors love that. If they only know one song they'll go and make fools of themselves in a way they wouldn't dream of doing at home.'

Martin chuckled as he spoke, but both agreed that when the audience was thin, there was something vital missing from the atmosphere. A full house put life and zest into the players and this was reflected in their playing.

Idris had been convicted of wilful damage to the company's coach and would be appearing before the magistrates court the following month. No point, mused Elizabeth now, in wasting sympathy on him or his mother. He was only getting his just deserts. Her blood boiled as she recalled his despicable behaviour when the coach had pulled up at the traffic lights. Seeing the whole orchestra assembled in that coach, and hating every one of them, he had surely aimed that horrible brick at Peter's head. If a son of hers behaved in that way she would be so ashamed that she would want to disappear off the face of the earth. But any son brought up in Swallow Tree Gardens would automatically have a cultured background, as well as good taste. Yes, any son of hers would be nurtured on the right lines so that nothing could go wrong.

Her mind flitted about as she listened to the soothing music. Her life would be more fulfilled if she did have a son. Yet, deep down, an awful doubt loomed that possibly she was too old to have another baby. People did say that twenty was preferable to thirty-five, and most of her friends' children were now at grammar school. They'd had their families young, when they hadn't a care in the world. If she started a baby now, would she be a burden both to herself and Roger? She'd read so much lately about side-effects and symptoms and all this talk about Downes Syndrome babies sounded most depressing. Yet the thought of actually having a child around the house again was most beguiling: one she found difficult to get out of her system.

It was a tremendous consolation that she and Roger had found each other after so long and could speak the same language. Somehow it was as if those six bleak years had never been. They never talked about them — for there was nothing to discuss. Roger had lived his life, thousands of miles away, and she had tried to live hers. The estrangement which developed had been out of her control. She couldn't help depriving Roger of her love, she reflected, nor of blaming him for Timothy's death. It was as if a needle had stuck in one groove of a record. She had pushed Roger out of her life, treating him almost like a stranger.

Elizabeth recalled endless winter mornings, with no visitors to get up for, when she had reluctantly opened her eyes, then tried to will herself back to sleep so as never to wake up again. How useless she had felt, how purposeless and inadequate! All day she had hoped nobody would call or phone, and if anybody in the street asked how she felt, she had said brightly: 'Oh fine, just fine,' and quickly changed the subject, because she hated talking about herself.

The music club had proved disappointing. She had hoped to lose herself in that, but the members were all too amateurish, too shallow. Knowing far more than they, she had missed the intellectual conversation she would so greatly have enjoyed had they been professionals. Then Peter Emmanual had come along as director of the orchestra and, as their friendship developed, her sea of despair had become a river of contentment. And since April, when Giovanni had entered her life, she had been treading on air, so that the mere sound of a violin, and particularly any excerpt from the Elgar Concerto, would send exhilarating thrills through every vein in her body.

The music ended, the clapping subsided, and the double doors opened for the interval. Immediately the impelling rhythm of a majestic brass band could be heard, floating over the sea from the bandstand, every note distinct and clear.

'An enormous band,' remarked Elizabeth, 'judging by the volume. There must be at least six trumpets and a whole host of drums.'

'Yes,' nodded Martin, 'and with what vigour they're playing those patriotic songs of Wales.'

At that moment Sylvia came tripping off stage to claim Martin so they could enjoy their coffee together. She was fingering her engagement ring as if to make sure it was there, her blue eyes sparkling as she gazed up at her fiance.

'What do you think, Martin?' Elizabeth overheard. 'Dr. Emmanual will be making a re-shuffle! Justin is leaving soon and going back to his teaching job, so he's going to switch you to cello and leave me on viola. Isn't it super? I just can't believe it!'

Martin looked puzzled as he tried to take this in. Then realizing it meant promotion for Sulvia, he looked equally delighted:

'That's fine! It looks as if we shall all be pleased. Even Richard should celebrate if he's getting a stand to himself.'

'Well, actually,' confessed Sylvia with a half laugh, 'Richard's been a lot nicer to me lately. He even gave me an engagement present today, a lovely set of serviettes in pale blue.'

101

In spite of the counter attraction and the scanty audience, Peter Emmanual seemed as cheerful as ever as Elizabeth carried her coffee over to join him at his table in the far corner. There was a bunch of papers scattered about in front of him and he was sorting them into piles.

'I've got the answer, Liz,' he greeted her heartily as she took a seat and sipped her coffee. 'I've got all these choirs lined up to compete in our Festival.'

'Why, that sounds great!' Elizabeth did her best to sound as enthusiastic as Peter. She had really joined him with a view to discussing Giovanni and the clinic, but first she must give in and, as always, listen patiently to his story:

'Our Festival of Choirs commences the first week in September. I've contacted all the local newspapers along the coast and they've promised me a wonderful build-up. There are fifty replies here, so I'm sorting out the ladies for Monday, men for Tuesday, mixed on Wednesday, and children's Thursday. That leaves Friday and Saturday for the finals and the grand finale.'

His voice was jubilant, like church bells at a wedding, his face ecstatic.

'It's all being organised so splendidly by the 'friends', Liz dear, and I'm so grateful. We must get silver cups for the winners and all sorts of prizes for the runners-up.'

'I can imagine how pleased you must be, Peter. It certainly will boost our audience and lengthen the season. It should make a big impact on the town. Can we talk about Giovanni?' Elizabeth went on. 'We must have a get-together about this clinic idea. We have to be sure we are doing the right thing.'

'I quite agree, my dear.' As he spoke, Peter fastened an elastic band round the bunch of papers and slipped them into his brief-case.

'If it suits you and Roger, I'll bring Dr. Weissman round to your place tomorrow, and we can all go into the matter thoroughly.'

'Shall we say two o'clock?'

Elizabeth thought it best to clinch the matter. The whole idea had become one of great urgency in her mind, and there were a few questions she was anxious to put to Dr. Weissman. So perhaps — with Gio's keenness, Roger's worldly wisdom and the doctor's detailed explanations — they would be able to come to a positive conclusion.

102

Chapter 13

'Be sure to write now . . .'

Elizabeth was handing an assortment of suitcases to Giovanni, already seated in the back seat of the luxurious Volkswagen. Her tone was anxious but, with an enormous effort, she maintained a smile.

'I will, Elizabeth. I'll put everything down on paper and send it straight off.' Gio's voice was calm and there was a certain serenity about his face.

'You can expect Roger and me in four weeks' time. We'll book in at a hotel so we can come and see you every day.'

She forced optimism into her voice and controlled the quivering of her lips. How fragile he looked, as though the air from the half-open window would blow him away. His dark curls were falling over his thin oval face and there was a placid contentment about his eyes.

She knew, with a sinking feeling, how very much she would miss him. Whatever happened now must be for the best — but the house would seem empty and there would be a vacuum in her heart, as if something vital were missing.

Giovanni had insisted on taking the new violin and his bunch of manuscripts. Tempted at one point to burst out to Roger the full story of the violin, she had, on second thoughts, decided to wait. Any criticism of her action apart, he might forbid such an expensive instrument to leave the house. So the dreadful conspiracy of silence about the violin remained, and whenever she thought about it Elizabeth still had twinges of guilt in the pit of her stomach.

'I'll be lost without these,' Gio had said and, with his usual charm and understanding smile, Dr. Weissman had agreed to making a space for them on the carpeted floor beside the boy's feet:

'He'll be a happier patient to deal with if he can pursue his hobby at my place. Nothing like a contented mind for a steady cure.'

Elizabeth did have qualms about the security of so valuable an instrument but, in view of the boy's tranquil expression, she put all mercenary ideas out of her mind and concentrated instead on getting Gio off to a cheerful start. She would then have the happy knowledge that he would have his music with him, although he would be many hundreds of miles away.

Peter had managed to get hold of a copy of the confidential medical papers from the file at the hospital, and she had written for the case history from the children's home. All these were, safely, stowed away in Gio's suitcases. He had been showered with presents from the members of the orchestra; black cats, horse shoes, lucky charms. Some had given him sensible gifts like warm pullovers, bed socks and wooly gloves. Roger had thrown in a lighthearted book full of jokes and general humour: 'You'll be amongst foreigners, Gio, and glad of an occasional laugh in your own language.' How understanding of him, Elizabeth had thought. Who else would have been so practical?

Peter had bought him a warm dressing gown in a colourful Welsh plaid, with matching fleecy lined slippers, while Elizabeth had given him a portable cassette player with a good supply of classical tapes, just what she herself would have wished for had she been going away like this.

The nicest part of all was when Gio thrust an oblong parcel into her hand at the very last minute.

'It's a Bible,' he said, with a slight tremor in his voice. 'I knew you needed one, and I've marked some of the passages you'll find helpful. It's only a little gift, Elizabeth. Nothing I gave you could fully express my gratitude for all your kindness . . .'

He broke off and then, in a practical tone, he continued, 'I'll phone from Dover tonight, and again after we've crossed the Channel. I'm so glad you gave me that photo of you and Roger in Swallow Tree Gardens. I shall treasure it more than anything else.'

As the foreign car drove away amidst laughter and fond fare-wells, with encouraging sounds from Dr. Weissman, Elizabeth was aware of a distinct feeling of relief. Something good *must* happen now. She must dismiss all those distressing thoughts of experiments and painful injections. Dr. Weissman seemed a pleasant enough man, if a trifle brisk. His motives were surely excellent. Without promising a cure, this unorthodox doctor had insisted that, under his treatment, Giovanni's life would at least be lengthened. Some of the symptoms would gradually diminish as the therapeutic remedies took full effect.

'A most interesting case,' was his catch phrase, 'and eminently worthy of investigation. When you come to my clinic, Frau Williams, you will see for yourself how much I have to offer my patients. Yes, something to offer sick people of which the medical world knows nothing — or to which it turns a blind eye. Auf Weidersehn, Frau and Herr Williams. I will see you in four weeks!'

True to his promise, Gio phoned at eleven o'clock. Elizabeth gathered that all had gone well so far. They were about to embark and would sail at midnight. With a silent prayer, she turned over the leaves of the glossy new Bible. He had marked the verse in the Epistle of Peter, 'casting all your cares upon Him, for He careth for you' and then again in Luke, 'the very hairs of your head are numbered. Fear not, therefore, for ye are of more value than many sparrows.'

Guiltily, and prayerfully, she closed the Bible. The boy was an example of faith and something would have to be done in her own life to increase her faith. How wonderful it must be to possess that same inner calm and tranquillity.

Re-opening the Bible, she read through to the end of the chapter. Then, with another silent prayer, she put out the light and drifted into a peaceful sleep.

* * *

'They'll have to bring in more chairs from the cafe.'

'Yes, and there are spare chairs in the bar that could come in here.'

'Just look at the crowd outside, all trying to push in! And a whole stream of them are still hurrying down the pier.'

There was a general hubbub in the Pier Head Pavilion, now full to overflowing, with not an empty seat in sight and everybody talking at the same time. What a wonderful start for Dr. Emmanual's Choir Festival.

Naomi joined Elizabeth, who had come specially early in order to claim her usual seat. Both surveyed the crowd already seated, with more crowds trying so hard to push in.

'There's a whole row standing up at the back,' marvelled Naomi, 'leaning against that wall. And my dear, look at all those children sitting cross-legged under the stage! I've never seen the place so full! They're crushed together like commuters on an underground train in the rush hour!'

The door keepers gained permission to leave the wide double doors open and accommodate the extended audience out on the pier on deck chairs, stools and benches. A feeling of excitement permeated the pavilion, everybody apparently on tiptoe with expectation.

'Let's hope this enthusiasm lasts the whole week,' Naomi remarked as she took off her white gloves and placed them in her handbag. 'This should put Peter in a good mood for the rest of the season. Why, there's the *Chronicle* reporter further down our row! If he gives a good report the whole town will know of our success.'

Peter Emmanual looked quite ten feet tall to Elizabeth's eyes as he strutted along the front of the stage. Having passed a satisfied glance over the rows and rows of fences, he surveyed his orchestra with as much vanity as a peacock showing off his feathers. Then he introduced the first item, a Rossini Overture, and the concert began.

The colourful souvenir programme which had been printed explained that, after two short items from the orchestra, the stage would be reserved for three choirs in turn, to render their items, the time being limited to twelve minutes for each. Then, after a Selection from *Lilac Time*, there would be an interval of ten minutes. Following that, three more ladies' choirs would compete. Then, while the judges compared notes, the orchestra would conclude with a pot-pourrie of Gilbert and Sullivan favourites.

Each choir had done its utmost to outdo the other choirs in performance and originality. Some of the dresses were distinguished, some outrageous, Elizabeth and Naomi agreed. The choir from Bethesda showed off the national Welsh dress to perfection with long flowing red gowns covered with crisp white aprons and tall black hats, all carrying baskets of eggs and oranges. A tiny child of three, dressed exactly the same, stood

106

like a mascot in front of the choir, her black hair and rosy cheeks giving her a doll-like appearance.

Everybody laughed as the Craigwen Choir walked on clad in skimpy green skirts showing purple legs and yellow shoes. Their original quip was a couple of guitar players instead of the usual piano accompaniment. The Bryn Morfydd Choir were the essence of sophistication, on the other hand, with delicate pink nylon gowns, long white gloves and pink rosebuds for head-dresses. Elizabeth and Naomi favoured the Victorian style, buttoned boots, long black gowns with lace pantaloons peeping out underneath, each girl holding a parasol. Their wide-brimmed hats were copiously trimmed with fruit and feathers. Their gimmick was a Welsh Harp accompaniment and, to Elizabeth, the ripple of chords sounded like a river flowing over smooth rocks on a hot summer's day.

Each choir sang with gusto, and the atmosphere was electric. One set of ladies did a ballerina effect, arms spread out gracefully to the rhythm of the singing, and a whole lot of dancing steps combined with the music.

It was a proud Dr. Emmanual who, at the end of the evening, presented the silver cup to the leader of the Bryn Morfydd Choir. Roars of applause and shouts of congratulations filled the hall as she walked off the stage in a swirl of delicate pink nylon, proudly holding the winning cup in her white gloved hands.

As Elizabeth made her way home, she felt relieved and more than happy that Peter's brainwave had so far proved such a success. She could well imagine the gleam in his eyes as he counted up the takings, and the press reports he would read with relish. The 'friends of the orchestra' would look forward to the following nights, hoping their pavilion would be just as full and the performance just as successful.

*　　*　　*　　*

'But Gretta — how can you be sure? This is a very serious accusation to make, you know!'

Elizabeth had been standing beside the sink, preparing vegetables. As a hysterical Gretta rushed in she had sat down quickly on a nearby stool, her face scarlet, her eyes flashing with anger.

'Es ist wahr. It is true, Mrs. Williams.'

Gretta was a pathetic figure as she stood in the open doorway

107

with tears rolling down both cheeks, her arms waving about distractedly.

'Der Vater ist Gio! But honestly it was no Liebschaft — no love affair, as you say.'

'How long have you known this? Does Gio know? Has your doctor confirmed it?'

The questions came tumbling out like lava from a volcano. There was both panic and alarm in Elizabeth's voice as she put out a hand to steady herself.

'It was mitleid, Mrs. Williams, nicht Liebe,' continued the unhappy girl. 'What do you say now, it was sympathy, not love. I was so sorry for him — my heart — it did ache. You remember it well. The days I was Krankenschwester to poor Gio — those days and nights that he lost all heart and was so very sad.'

Gretta flopped into a chair, holding her head with both hands as she sobbed:

'My mother and my father throw me out — strict and stern, they are. I am desperate, Mrs. Williams.'

As the truth of this dreadful story penetrated, Elizabeth's vision blurred. How on earth could Gio, in his low state of health, have become the father of a child in this way? He was neither especially interested in girls nor the sort to make advances of this kind. Could it be that Gretta was making a scapegoat of him in order to clear herself? No, the more the girl told her, the more she had to force herself to accept the truth.

It all fitted in. The dates added up. Gretta had been told at the surgery that same morning that she could expect the child about the middle of April.

Gretta related to Elizabeth, between sobs, how terribly sorry she had felt for Gio at the time when he had fallen apart with grief. She had fussed him, circling her arms around his thin weak body and holding him close, just as a mother would comfort a sick child. How unfair it had all seemed to her that, while she was healthy and strong, with all her life before her, this poor innocent boy had been given only six months to live. Gretta spoke then of how he had crept to her room in the middle of the night for sympathy, and had then remained beside her till the sun came streaming through the curtains as the alarm clock sounded at seven.

It all fitted inescapably into place. So this was the reason for Gretta's lack of energy! No wonder the girl had changed so dramatically and been so reluctant to come down to the aroma of fried bacon and sausages.

There was certainly a problem here. If her parents were so strict and religious there could be no question of an abortion. In her present state of mind, Gretta seemed reluctant to write to them. How long would she be able to help in the dining room? She was so good at dealing with the guests, she knew every aspect of the work, and had turned out to be a real treasure to Elizabeth. Indeed she had brought with her an air of jollity and breeziness into the somewhat sober atmosphere of the busy guest house.

This problem would affect a number of people. The question was just how to deal with it. Elizabeth, responsible for Gretta as an au pair girl, would be obliged to see it through and help her in the best possible way.

The question remained . . . how?

Chapter 14

'I have good news to report. The picture has not looked so rosy for a long time. We now have a large surplus in our funds.'

Peter Emmanual was addressing a 'coffee morning' at the Dutch Cafe, the perfect place for a get-together of this kind, their scones were so delicious. It made an interesting treat for the fifty or so dedicated people who came regularly to support him. He would give all the news in his usual witty style, thank them for their efforts, and set forth his future plans.

Elizabeth and Naomi had taken a window seat overlooking the shopping centre. Their eyes rested not on the crowd of holiday makers ambling by, but on Peter Emmanual's eager features as he continued:

'Our Festival of Choirs may well be an annual event, ladies and gentlemen. We have got off to an excellent start and there is no reason that I can see why we should not continue in the same way. Many thanks to you all for your unfailing help and valuable support. And now Elizabeth will tell you about some forthcoming events, in particular the bring and buy sale.'

Peter sat down heavily beside his spouse, who, with an approving look, offered him a wedge of Black Forest Gateau.

Elizabeth pointed out that she would need help in manning the various stalls, stationery, toiletry and gifts, as usual, with a large table for home-made cakes, jams and chutneys. This year they would be including a section for books, tapes and records, and it was hoped this would prove profitable.

Once again the doctor rose to his feet. With the funds looking so healthy, they were now in a position to offer the council a more realistic rent for the hire of the pavilion. Also if some of the 'friends' took over the cafe in the interval, the regular staff could get away much sooner. He spoke of a petition being circulated to every home in the area, a petition that the Palm Court Orchestra should continue to play and every effort should be made to retain the town's unique Victorian atmosphere.

Naomi and Elizabeth exchanged a few words at the end of the session. The Festival had indeed been a week to remember, they agreed. Hundreds of spectators had arrived in coach loads from all over North Wales to support the competitors, and had gone away with a good report. Thursday had proved the most popular night, with hundreds of doting parents taking their places as near as possible to the stage to see their children performing.

'I never saw so many little legs in white socks and sandals,' said Naomi, 'tripping off that stage escorted by all those proud teachers.'

'Nor so many fresh young faces,' Elizabeth added. 'Their youthful voices radiated such warmth, didn't they, as they tried to please the judges?'

'And the reporters and photographers had a field day! So many cameras clicking, so many questions fired at the youngsters to make a good story for the *Weekly News.*'

Yet, deep down, Elizabeth still entertained doubts about the whole thing. All very well for Peter to stand there talking about the festival becoming an annual event. Surely he was caught up in a wave of optimism — viewing everything through rose-coloured spectacles? The excessive praise of his admirers must have gone to his head! He knew well enough that half of the town council were still violently opposed to his classical music. And still Zechariah Jones was doing his utmost to push him out altogether.

She would have to spell it out to Peter when they were alone. One swallow certainly didn't make a summer, she would argue, and their orchestra had a long way to go to gain the confidence of the whole town. There could be hectic scenes at next month's council meeting when the fixtures for next season were discussed.

Another setback was the absence of Giovanni. Since his illness a lot of local people had stopped coming to the concerts and it would be almost impossible to find such an attraction again; such brilliance, such superb playing and all within the space of twelve weeks. April, May and June had taken the music lovers by storm. Giovanni had made his name, and now it looked as if this was all over. Now it was cello solos, or a woodwind

111

quartet, and instead of Giovanni leading the orchestra in his youthful flamboyant style, Peter stood there, middle-aged and greying, conducting, leading and playing, and it wasn't the same at all.

Elizabeth still hadn't got round to telling Roger about the new violin. It would demand rather more courage than she possessed at the moment. He was quite a dear about most things — but how might he react to her impulsive expenditure of the central heating money? If only she had told him sooner! She could only hope he would see it her way. The very fact that the boy had always longed for an Italian violin was fair enough, but it became an even more deserving case when he was given only six months to live. If poor Giovanni was dead at the end of that time, she would sell it back to the shop and there would be no problem. But she really must bring herself to tell Roger about it, particularly as several people already knew; she would hate him to hear about it from other source.

Then there was the problem of Gretta nagging at the back of her mind. Only that morning she had tried to talk in a motherly way to the poor girl.

'I — I feel so bad about it, Mrs. Williams. I almost say to myself that I will go for an abortion and keep it all dark, as you English say.'

Gretta's voice had broken involuntarily, her eyes full of tears. Horrified at the very idea, Elizabeth had pointed out, as gently as she could, the possible side-effects to her emotions and general health. Also it could affect her ability to have more children later on.

'But you know what they do to me, Mrs. Williams? In a convent I go, a Kloster as we say. My cousin was so. She stay there two year and change so much in that time. That is something I do not want.' The image of Gretta's tear-stained face was on Elizabeth's mind as she fell into a troubled sleep.

It was in the middle of the night that the idea struck with force. Sitting bolt upright she stared at the bedside clock, which registered three a.m. Her mind had started to work on a plan. A scheme was being set into motion. Could it work? And would Roger agree?

To adopt this baby as her own . . . that was the obvious answer! So obsessed did she become by the idea that she felt an urge to go along and talk to Gretta about it, or else wake up

Roger and put it to him. She felt fully awake, brimming over with energy, bristling with plans. Twenty or so visitors were asleep in various parts of the house: she must be careful not to wake them.

In the inky hush of the night, she crept mouselike down the carpeted stairs to the kitchen, hoping that a cup of hot tea would calm her restless spirit. She half expected to meet Gretta on the way. Telepathy is a queer thing and, after all, they shared the same problem. It would have seemed natural to see Gretta's nimble figure flit along the landing.

But there was no sound and, after her second cup of delicious strong tea, she crept back to lie silently beside Roger, with wide open eyes, till dawn.

'You really mean it, Liz? You yourself would take on that baby?'

Roger, reaching for dressing gown and slippers, stared at his wife in amazement. Elizabeth had drawn back the curtains and, wearing her pink nylon negligé, stood by the open window, pretending to admire the garden.

'That's right.' She swung round to face him, her eyes bright with expectancy. 'If we adopted it from the start, Roger dear, it would be like having our own child.'

She sat beside him on the bed, squeezing his arm as she gazed up into his face. 'It would be a practical way of solving Gretta's problem. And, believe me, Roger, it *is* a problem.'

'A bit drastic, luv. Supposing we have our own baby straight away?' Roger sounded doubtful and there was a pucker like a frown between his eyes.

Trust her husband to be practical and down to earth! The possibility had struck Elizabeth and, of course, had to be faced. But she was not to be easily put off.

'If that happened there would be two babies instead of one and we could bring them up as twins.'

'You'd be taking on something there, Liz. We've no idea of the background of either of the parents. Taking on other people's babies . . . isn't it rather risky?'

'We do know them both; it's not like going to an orphanage and getting just any baby. Look at Gretta: her zest for life! She sweeps everyone along, doesn't she, Roger, on a tide of enthusiasm and fun? She's healthy, she's jolly and she's young. Then

113

look at Gio. Surely his child will be a born musician from the start. The background's there all right. I see no problems.'

'Needs plenty of thinking about if you ask me. We would have to be sure, very sure, before we committed ourselves. Have you said anything to Gretta?'

'Of course not, I wouldn't say a word till I'd asked you first,' Elizabeth blurted out. 'We'll put it to her as soon as we've made up our minds and see how she reacts. The idea sounds simply marvellous to me — Gio's child here in this house, with his father's musical genius in his veins. Oh Roger, what a glorious thing to happen!'

Lighthearted and excited, Elizabeth tugged at her husband's arm, pulled him to the centre of the floor and started waltzing round the bedroom.

Now I've told Roger, she mused, and he didn't exactly decline. If I go about it in the right way, with a bit of tact and persuasion and plenty of manipulation, he'll come round in the end; he always does. My next hurdle is to break it to Gretta and get her to see it as the obvious way out. I must write to her parents and promise to look after their daughter as if she were my own until the baby is born.

Gretta accepted the idea at once but insisted upon Elizabeth writing to explain to her parents.

'Well, if you say so, Gretta dear, but I'll need your help with the language. My letter can be a long one and I promise no blame will be attached to you: I will take the blame for this. Now get the dictionary, will you? Then we can start putting our thoughts down on paper in the best German we can.'

'Ja! Ja!' The girl put her arms around Elizabeth and hugged her. 'Das ist gut. But one thing I wish, that we do not say this to Gio. He is too troubled already. He will not want to know this.'

Chapter 15

Whenever the postman came Elizabeth expected something from Gio. Fourteen days had seemed a long time to wait, but when three weeks passed without a word, she began to feel uneasy. He had promised faithfully to write and tell her everything. He was not the type to break his word. So what could have gone wrong?

There was time to talk to Roger these days. Apart from one honeymoon couple there were only two elderly ladies, so the dining room looked almost empty and Elizabeth and Roger could enjoy a leisurely breakfast together before the guests came down.

'Has it occurred to you that we have no actual proof Dr. Weissman is a practitioner — or even that he is genuine?' Elizabeth's face registered her acute anxiety as she poured out her thoughts to Roger over their egg and bacon. 'Frankly, I sometimes wonder if we haven't been conned. Anybody can produce a glossy brochure. What evidence do we have that everything is above board?'

'I wouldn't worry, luv. Foreign posts aren't always reliable at this time of year: some letters take as long as three weeks. Give the boy time to get his bearings. After all, he's in a weak state and entered the place as a complete stranger in a foreign land.'

The ring of optimism in Roger's voice was, Elizabeth sensed, put on for her benefit.

'One thing I've thought of since he went. Isn't it odd, looking back, the number of different treatments this man suggested? Fancy including faith-healing with acupuncture. And why incorporate psychiatry with yoga and meditation? It doesn't really mix.' Elizabeth sighed heavily as she poured her second cup of coffee.

'The way I see it, luv, he's spreading the net far and wide to appeal to different types of patient. By so doing he gets them all in.'

Roger's tone was slow and deliberate. Clearly he was bent upon appearing as if there was nothing to panic about.

'Like being two-faced, you mean, or being all things to all men?'

Elizabeth pushed her cooked breakfast on one side. All this looked dreadfully suspicious. Hadn't she ensured that Gio had enough foreign coins to be able to phone her, and also a supply of stationery? She really should have had some communication by now.

Only the previous day she had spent a frustrating forty minutes trying to telephone the clinic. After getting the engaged tone several times, she had used her limited knowledge of the language in order to check the number with directory enquiries. She had been given another number to try and this time it had sounded like the out-of-order tone. Then she had tried the first number again and a faint far away German voice had come through: 'Bitte schon. Bitte schon. Ein minuten.' Heart thumping, fingers trembling she had hung on as the expensive minutes ticked away. Finally, still with no response, she had hung up more despondent than ever.

Desperate thoughts of kidnapping entered Elizabeth's mind. Could Dr. Weissman have schemed some sort of trick whereby he got hold of Gio in order to carry out his tests for the benefit of his other patients? Was he a doctor at all? Could it not be an unscrupulous hoax to get hold of an attractive young boy for some underhand purpose? Why, oh *why*, didn't Gio write or phone, just to say all was well?

There was a tang of Autumn in the air, the high winds blowing twigs off the trees into the field behind Swallow Tree Gardens. At high tide huge frothy waves beat against the sea wall and tumbled over on to the promenade. In anorac and jeans, Gretta joined Elizabeth on short country walks, along the field paths, through the woods and around the Marine Drive. Gretta had been keen to gather mushrooms for breakfast and blackberries for jam and pies. Elizabeth was overjoyed that she had accepted the idea of having the baby, and of spending the winter at Swallow Tree Gardens. It was as if a cloud had been lifted; her serious expression was replaced by sparkling eyes, a ready smile and her usual infectious laugh.

Her father would agree to the plan, Gretta confided, but she had doubts about her mother, who had such hopes of her only child becoming head librarian at the central library in Munich. The news of the pregnancy would come as a shock to her mother because it would interrupt her education by preventing her from starting university.

Roger had spent almost a thousand pounds on getting himself a new gun, and several hundred pounds on his share in a syndicate for shooting rights on a large estate in Anglesey. This went some way towards relieving Elizabeth's conscience about the twelve thousand pounds paid out for the violin; particularly as she still had not admitted to him what she had done. What made it worse was the fear, at times, that she might never see Gio or the violin again. One whole month seemed a terribly long time to wait for even a brief communication.

Good tempered though he was on the surface, Roger could still get roused if anything displeased him. Elizabeth still had not forgotten that dreadful night when he had first come in contact with Gio. Would he call her a fool, or incompetent, or not fit to handle money? And what if the violin should be lost for good? It would be such a pity if their restored relationship were to be spoiled, and so she postponed the evil moment as long as she could.

The one bright prospect which sustained Elizabeth was the thought that by next April she would be holding Gio's child in her arms, cuddling and feeding him or her. What a perfect idea it sounded! If only April would come sooner, her heartache would pass. It was like a fantasy about to come true. She allowed her mind to dip into the future, conjuring up happy pictures of ideal family life such as she had often dreamed about.

Elizabeth hadn't reckoned with the dramatic response of Frau Deutchtung to the news contained in her letter. The arrival of a taxi and the sudden peel of the front door bell, then the unexpected appearance of the woman on her door step; all this came as a complete surprise. It was three o'clock and the house was quiet, but the explosion which followed was an encounter Elizabeth could well have done without.

She recognised in the face a mature version of Gretta's, but instead of the girl's natural sparkle and gaiety, there was a distinctly frozen expression. Frau Deutchtung was so dressed that she looked as if she had been gift-wrapped. She wore a fur stole over a sleek silk dress in powder blue, which emphasised the curves of an ample figure. Her plump made-up face was defiant yet pretty, the brilliant patches of rouge on her cheeks making them appear enflamed. Her neck and wrists were heavy with flashy jewellery and on her head perched a provocative little hat decorated with flowers, fruit and feathers. Short brown hair, slightly grey, stood up in symmetrical waves around her head and she carried an aura of expensive perfume. She waved her arms about, emphasising every word in broken English laced with explosive German:

'I vill not vaste time, Frau Villiams!' Her penetrating eyes were fixed on Elizabeth's, her face scarlet with rage. 'I get straight to dee point! I am not happy about my girl and your very bad letter to me.'

Elizabeth's heart did a double somersault. Whatever had gone wrong now? That careful explanatory letter, composed so cleverly by Gretta and herself, first in English and then, with the girl's help, in German, should have cleared up the problem! This woman would get her daughter back within six months, minus the baby, and all would be well. And yet, she realised, Frau Deutchtung was about to ruin everything. First she had better get this woman, seething with rage, off the street and into the privacy of the lounge.

'Do come inside, Frau Deutchtung,' she said smoothly, 'no point standing out here in the cold. I'll put the kettle on. You must have travelled a long way today.'

'You tell me last January,' rattled on Frau Deutchtung now seated uneasily in one of the lounge chairs. Her shrill voice resounded through the house. 'You tell me that you look after my liebing and care for her as if at home. And now you tell me she is to have a child and you wish to have it for yourself. A trick it is, Frau Villiams. Ah yes, I see it all! You vish for a child yourself, and so you use my daughter!'

'Really, Frau Deutchtung!' Elizabeth instilled a note of severity into her voice. 'You must not jump to ridiculous conclusions! I promised to care for Gretta for the summer season — but who can watch a teenage girl every minute of the day? She has to live. I did try my best, Frau Deutchtung. I gave her a good home, as she herself will tell you . . .'

118

'Vhere is my Gretta now? Vhere is my child? I insist that she pack her things. And then ve go!'

Elizabeth knew exactly where Gretta was and told her mother in a mixture of simple English and her own limited knowledge of German. That morning Gretta had seen in the paper a recipe for blackberry crumble in the true Welsh style. This had impelled her to go off on the mountain with a plastic bowl. Knowing exactly where a good supply of ripe fruit was to be found, she was relishing the fun of making the crumble herself for the evening meal.

Elizabeth felt safe about Gretta and knew she had her confidence. But this unreasonable mother of hers was quite a different matter. Clutching at straws and, as a last resort, putting as much authority into her voice as her nerves would allow, she exclaimed:

'I suggest we let Gretta decide for herself, Frau Deutchtung. It's her life and she's old enough to know her own mind. She ought to be allowed . . .'

'Schund!' broke in Frau Deutchtung. 'Rubbish! My girl do as I say. I take her now and she spend this time in a Kloster and the baby is theirs. I tell you also, Frau Villiams, that the International Society shall know about this terrible thing. Yes, I shall report you! You will hear more of this. It is 'court-case' as you say.'

Elizabeth explained that she had suggested the girl stay in North Wales in her own interests. Surely it was better to keep her pregnancy a secret from friends and relations in Germany? In just over six months Gretta would be free to resume her studies and home again as if nothing had happened.

It was at this point that Gretta herself appeared, her weather-beaten face aglow as she thrust her bowl of luscious blackberries into Elizabeth's lap. Then, as she saw her mother sitting there, her expression changed to one of shock, almost amounting to fear. Elizabeth tactfully left them alone as they embraced and greeted one another.

Waiting for the kettle to boil, she laid a dainty tray for Frau Deutchtung, hoping against hope that some miracle would occur and a cup of strong tea would solve all the difficulties.

Much shouting could now be heard from the lounge, in German too quick for Elizabeth to follow. Gretta was clearly arguing against her mother's idea, but the older woman's aggressive voice predominated and Elizabeth's heart sank: this could mean the end of her dream of having Gio's child. The woman was doing her level best to ruin everything!

Returning to the lounge with her tray, Elizabeth found Gretta alone, staring into space. Frau Deutchtung had stormed off, it seemed, declining the offer of tea and cakes.

'My mother has gone,' Gretta whimpered. 'Booked in at Regent Palace Hotel. She come back tomorrow, told me to pack and be ready to go. It's so awful, Mrs. Williams, so terrible . . . How shall I leave you?'

Elizabeth sat down beside the stricken girl and put her arms round her. 'Don't cry any more. Just drink this tea, my sweet one.'

Sounding far more cheerful than she felt, she poured out two cups of tea and coaxed Gretta to try a home-made cake:

'There must be a way out. Shall we make it a praying matter? If we both pray earnestly tonight, who knows? Something may well turn up.'

Her optimism was put on for effect, for she could honestly think of no way in which the difficulty might be solved.

Always, Gretta confided, her mother had been a strong minded person who could never stand the slightest opposition. She would move heaven and earth to get her own way.

It was comforting to know that Gretta was on her side, and wished with all her heart to stay at Swallow Tree Gardens, to book a bed in Bangor Maternity Hospital and enjoy the winter in the seclusion of North Wales, away from all those people at home.

But it was a sad Elizabeth who finally dozed off with Frau Deutchtung's final words ringing in her ears:

'I take my child home. To a convent she go . . . and the baby is theirs!'

Chapter 16

Pre-occupied with nagging thoughts of Gio so far away, and distracted with worries about Gretta, Elizabeth still forced herself to glance through *The Times Educational Supplement* as usual. Her eyes widened as she saw an insertion in bold black type. It concerned the uses for the Technical College extension, four miles along the coast, and the message seemed to her of vital importance.

Knowing Gretta was in bed and Roger 'out with the boys', she grabbed coat and handbag — although the clock said well past ten o'clock — stuffed the page from *The Times* into her bag, and made for Peter Emmanual's house.

'Great news, Peter!' she exclaimed as the musical director helped her off with her coat before ushering her into his comfortable lounge. 'Just look at this in the *Times Educational Supplement*. Here, in bold black letters . . . what we've all been waiting for!'

Eyes shining, she thrust the whole page into his face.

' 'Plans for the new extension', ' he read out in a deadpan tone.

'Yes, and plans for the new syllabus! It's ideas they're after, Peter. See what it says.' Impatiently she grabbed the paper back. 'It says they've allowed for languages and sciences in that new wing, and now they're looking for suggestions from tutors. We have to write to the Education Authority in Caernarvon, giving details of all suggested subjects and Mr. Islwyn Vaughan is the man we have to write to. Oh, it's fabulous — nothing short of a miracle! Can't you see yourself as head of a huge music section in that college, with students coming from all over, and the boys from your orchestra teaching there?'

'You really think so, Liz?'

Peter, lighting his cigar, sat further back in his luxurious arm-chair and blew a spiral of blue smoke into the air.

'Of course I think so! We must get in quick if we are to be the first in the field. You should get preferential treatment because you live here and — with all your qualifications — it's as good as settled.'

'Have you thought out what we could say?'

His tone rather more hopeful now, Peter took the paper from Elizabeth and read the whole column.

'The main thing is to offer them your experience in the field of music. Then we could mention how much a music section is needed in this area — work on the fact that there's no classical music between here and Bangor.'

'But first, shouldn't we ask the boys in the orchestra what they think?'

'Don't wait for that!' Just playing for time, Elizabeth sensed with suppressed impatience. 'By the time you've contacted them all and obtained their sanction, somebody else will have got in first. I'll tell you what: we'll draft a letter now. You sign one of your letterheads and I'll go home and type it out and catch the first post in the morning.'

Driving home around midnight with the drafted letter in a long white envelope, she pondered that this bright spot had certainly made her day. Why, even Gretta's mother had been forgotten in the excitement of this new project! To think they would be able to find posts for the members of the orchestra, permanent jobs so they need not join the dole queue all winter. How inspiring it would be to have their own orchestra with students to bolster it up, and classical music all the year round.

The only point which worried her was the fact that not once during her visit had Peter mentioned Gio. Did he not share her anxiety over the boy? Was Gio just a name on his list of artistes, the ones who helped to boost his ego as they appeared on his stage?

It was an awful thought, but it appeared to be true.

*   *   *   *

A very different Frau Deutchtung arrived at Swallow Tree Gardens the following morning. Here was not the bombastic, noisy creature of the previous day, but a calm, restrained woman with very little to say. Elizabeth offered morning coffee, then left mother and daughter alone, enjoining them to talk as long as they wished. Curious about the transformation, she felt it must be a good omen and, with no raised voices reaching her ears, her heart became lighter as she smoothed out the tray cloth and reached for the best coffee pot.

A few minutes later an over-joyed Gretta rushed through to her:

'It is all right, Mrs. Williams! My mother is willing that I stay.'

'Really, Gretta? What splendid news!' This was indeed an unexpected turn of events, she thought. And aloud: 'Now calm down, and tell me all about it.'

It appeared that the previous evening Frau Deutchtung had shared a table at the Regent Palace Hotel with a couple from Germany, sad and broken-hearted after the death of their only daughter of seventeen.

They had related the story over the evening meal. Heidi had fallen madly in love with a local farm labourer. She had been working as an au-pair girl in a hotel, where she had come in contact with this good-looking, soft spoken Welsh boy. They had become engaged and planned to marry straight away. With a whole year to wait for her eighteenth birthday, she had sought her parents' permission, but they had flatly refused. 'We expect more from you, my girl,' they had flung at her. 'This Welsh farm worker is not your type: it is pure infatuation. When you come home and take up the threads of your own social circle you'll find a man more suitable.'

Time and time again Heidi had pleaded with them via long, expensive phone calls, but each time they had been adamant. To the poor girl the position must have indeed looked hopeless as she contemplated the prospect of life without Goronwy. The anguish of heart proving too much for her, she had taken an overdose of sleeping tablets and been found in a coma in her bedroom the following morning. Her parents, sent for immediately, had arrived at the hospital to find the stomach pump taken away, Heidi dead, and poor Goronwy weeping over her.

'If only we had agreed,' lamented the grief-stricken mother. 'We would have got used to him in time and have loved him for her sake. We shall always blame ourselves for this.'

Frau Deutchtung had not failed to note the haunted expression about the woman's eyes, the look of guilt and self-recrimination.

'We made a dreadful mistake,' put in the father gruffly. 'Take my advice, Frau Deutchtung, and never go against your daughter's wishes. Girls know their own mind. What would we not now give to see our little Heidi laughing and singing like she used to? A daughter has a right to live her own life.'

This tragic episode had done the trick. Gretta told Elizabeth the sad tale just as her mother had told her. The sequel was even more remarkable and Elizabeth glowed with delight when she realised just how everything had fallen into place. Frau Deutchtung had been tormented all that night by a dreadful nightmare: her poor Gretta lying dead in the bed beside her, dead of a broken heart.

The morning light had left her in no doubt whatever that Gretta must be allowed to have her own way over the baby. Whatever she had vowed before, she must now fall in line with Mrs. Williams' scheme. On no account could she risk a tragedy like that of poor Heidi.

'So you see, Mrs. Williams, we did right to pray! We now have our answer.' A beaming Gretta danced about the kitchen. 'Life in this house with you will be wunderbar. Danke schon. Du bist sehr gut.'

Elizabeth was quick to welcome a subdued Frau Deutchtung as a guest at Swallow Tree Gardens any time she chose. Gretta would be left alone when she and Roger made their promised visit to Switzerland. What a perfect opportunity for the two Deutchtungs to come and stay for the whole fortnight. It was the perfect solution. She and Roger could set off for Switzerland with an easy conscience, free from worry about Gretta.

* * * *

'That smells good, Liz. I say, the air on these Jura Mountains makes me as hungry as a hunter. Those sausages look most appetising. I can manage two eggs, by the way.'

Roger appeared in the chalet doorway, a picture of health and vitality in his track-suit and trainers. Elizabeth had heard him get out of his bunk-bed around six. Then she had snuggled down into her sleeping bag for another two hours, the faint jingling of cow bells soothing her back into peaceful slumber.

'We've not done Switzerland before of course. That's Lake Lausanne down there, luv, and if you look far enough you can see all Montreux spread out below. There's lots of bilberries up there on the mountain high above the conifers, and we'll have time to explore along this mountain path while we're here.'

'It really is superb, darling,' Elizabeth nodded with an affectionate smile as she handed him his breakfast plate. 'Wasn't it kind of Dr. Weissman to offer us a chalet? So much more homely than a stuffy hotel.'

As Roger tackled his breakfast with all the gusto of a ravenous schoolboy, she added: 'A good thing we brought our own food. I can see we shall need every bit of it. I know you prefer English breakfasts, and I guess you've earned that one.'

They sat on pinewood benches surveying the countryside, and Roger reached for a third slice of toast:

'I can't think how the patients in that clinic exist on all that green stuff! After lunch with them yesterday, I felt like crawling into the nearest rabbit hole.'

His face alight with eagerness, he went on to explain some of the plans he had in mind. These included climbing, rough walking and swimming.

Both had been amazed at the vastness of the Health Clinic, or Dr. Weissman's Medical Institution, as it was described in the brochure.

The clinic was spread over five acres and consisted of three separate and distinct buildings. Elizabeth and Roger had entered the wrong one on arrival and found difficulty in making themselves understood. With no sign of Dr. Weissman and nobody on duty in Reception, they had wasted an hour wandering along the labyrinth of corridors, balconies and sun lounges spread out on five floors. They meandered through cloisters with large areas of fresh green grass and an abundance of clean fresh air, which smelt like pine trees. Still finding nobody to ask, they had eventually made their way back to Reception, where a dark-haired girl was thumbing through a huge book, rapidly turning over its pages. Roger thought she looked like a nurse, but Elizabeth was sure, in view of her jogging suit and tennis pumps, that she must be a physical training teacher.

'Dr. Weissman is away at Berne for the morning, sir,' the girl replied, Roger having made an enquiry in a slow simple English tone. 'He vill be back in time for the Mittagessen.'

Elizabeth explained to Roger that this meant lunch. 'Surely

125

the boy we are looking for is here?' she exclaimed. 'Giovanni Malvolio, from Great Britain?'

'Gio? I know now who you mean, madam, and he is still in the first building, Das Landhaus Schlicht.'

The German girl could manage English very well, especially when she was explaining about the clinic. As she continued, Elizabeth hung on every word:

'Das Landhaus Schlicht is the place they go to for peace and quietness, and they have that for six weeks. It makes them calm and adaptable, you see. 'The quiet place', it mean in your language.'

What a wonderful thought, Elizabeth reflected. A place of quietness . . . how ideal it sounded for anybody just arriving with problems of health and nerves and such like. This foreign voice, rich with authority had already calmed her spirit. Gio was actually there, and before long she would see him.

The German girl had by now found the correct reference in the big register and was studying the pencil notes against his name.

'You see, Mr. and Mrs. Williams,' she continued, 'when they are in this quiet place they get a solitude which often is a cure in itself. After six weeks they come to my building, 'Das Landhaus Ubung', which means exercise and activity. It is my work to give them sport and Yoga, swimming and jogging, as you say. This build them up strong. In my building they get different food, nut savouries and cheese, with all kinds of vegetables and fruit.'

If only she could catch a glimpse of Gio, Elizabeth thought, her mind would now be completely at ease.

The girl was speaking again: 'At the end of my regime, they go to another mansion where Dr. Weissman works. There they have tests and inspection again, like when they first come in, and he make positive sure they are well enough for home. So, Frau Williams, we will now make this small journey to find your boy. We shall go through this gate, along this path into the woods, by the lake, and the next lane will lead to the right place for you.'

As Roger took Elizabeth's arm and they followed the nurse, she realised what a tower of strength her husband was at a time like this. She would have hated to be there alone, so strange did it all look. And yet even in its strangeness there was a distinct air of efficiency about the whole establishment which pleased them both.

The elevator in the 'Landhaus Schlicht' seemed to go on for ever, but finally it jerked them out on the level for Giovanni's ward. This lay at the end of a lengthy corridor with huge sliding windows on each side overlooking luscious green grass below. Opening a door, the nurse let them in, and at once Elizabeth gasped with delight: there was her Gio sitting beside an open window, his small flushed face quite serene. On seeing the newcomers, his expression became as sharp as a needle. Rushing towards them, he put both arms round Elizabeth, whose body filled with a surge of happiness as she realised how groundless all her fears had been.

'Gio, thank God you're all right! We've been worried about you . . .' She stood back, looking him up and down with shining eyes.

'There was no need for you to worry.' Gio looked puzzled. 'I told you everything was OK.'

'We hadn't heard anything for what seemed an awful long time.'

'But — I wrote to you the first week I was here! I wrote six whole pages, Elizabeth, and gave the letter with money for stamps to Heinz, who was going into the next building. I never saw him again . . . So you never got that letter?' His face clouded as he realised the position. 'I wrote again last week, though, and that letter will be at your house now. We are very restricted here: we do not mix with the world, as you might say.'

Giovanni laughed as he spoke and Elizabeth understood at once what he implied. Here, for the sake of solitude, they were cut off from the rest of the clinic, with no radio, no television, no telephone or even newspapers. It all sounded part of a perfect cure and both Elizabeth and Roger were impressed.

Scanning the room, she noticed the slippers and dressing gown from Peter, and the portable cassette player which she had given him. Also she couldn't fail to see an open Bible on his table, a book of prayers and a hymn book.

During their half-hour stay Gio told them all about his routine. As he spoke Elizabeth watched his face, his eyes, his breathing, and noted his tone of voice. Nothing escaped her as she listened intently:

'The accent is on fresh air, Elizabeth, and absolutely fresh raw food. They talk a lot about mineral salts and trace elements. Most of the vegetables come straight from the garden and are either minced or liquidised. We get a whole lot of fruit too. Then, four times a day, I take this herbal stuff that tastes bitter as gall. Somehow I swallow it and it burns its way all down me. It's a concentrated herbal preparation, intended to put back into the blood what is missing.'

'We start the day with prayers,' he continued, 'and Brother Herman and Brother Ernst are just right for that. It's a sobering way to begin each day. It puts you in the right mood for positive thinking, as they call it. Then I have to do deep breathing exercises in front of this open window. It's so pure and clean, you can smell the pine trees and the heather. I have to take a huge breath and count to twenty, and that helps the blood along. And there's something you'll appreciate, Elizabeth. During the period for relaxation and meditation, we get one whole hour of classical music. What a treat that is!'

All this time Roger sat on the other side of the ward, weighing up the landscape and the shapes of the mountains. Overjoyed that Elizabeth should at last have relaxed, he sat there half listening, content in the knowledge that all was not lost.

Elizabeth, for her part, glowed as she realised what faith Gio had in the treatment. It was with an extra bounce in her step that she returned along the white corridors with Roger's protecting arm around her.

They found Dr. Weissman waiting for them in Reception. He and his wife invited them to lunch at two o'clock, and Elizabeth was reassured to learn that he nourished great hopes of effecting a cure. Giovanni must continue with the herbal mixture for a very long time, he warned, and show great patience and courage.

'I really can see a light at the end of the tunnel,' the doctor concluded, 'albeit a tiny one, and quite a long way off.'

Chapter 17

The winter seemed long, as winters do at seaside resorts, with no visitors about and nothing much going on. But that winter was destined to have its moments.

The happiest one of all for Elizabeth was the day of Gio's discharge from the clinic. It was a crisp cold day at the beginning of March when Dr. Weissman wrote to say that, with care and attention, the boy could now live a normal life. He must follow the strict diet, and continue to take the herbal preparation, and must come back to Switzerland for a check-up in three months.

It so happened that the same week Gretta was admitted into hospital at Bangor. So the two never met, and Elizabeth was saved the embarrassment she had feared.

Gio improved rapidly from that day forward and it comforted Elizabeth to see more colour in his cheeks and more flesh on his body than ever she had seen before. His diet was not difficult and she went to great pains to get hold of every conceivable salad ingredient and present it as attractively as possible.

Gio explained to her that he had not wasted his spare time during the weeks in Switzerland, but had continued his violin practice and his composing. She was thrilled to hear that Dr. Peter Emmanual had arranged for him to play the Elgar Concerto at the Royal Festival Hall in two weeks time. Four front row seats were already reserved for himself and his wife, and for Roger and Elizabeth.

What a night of nights it proved to be; truly an occasion she would remember for the rest of her life. She still experienced the same thrill when Gio played. Gravely ill though he had been, he could still wield his bow expertly over the strings and produce a tone even more golden than before. Elizabeth realised what a difference the genuine Italian violin made as his audience remained as if spell bound, every eye upon his face, every ear responsive to the brilliance of his performance. There was no doubt about it, his whole soul went that night into his interpretation of this, the longest of all violin concertos, fully one hour in length. After three curtains, there was a standing ovation and the prolonged clapping continued long after he had left the stage for the fourth time.

Within three months Giovanni had given similar performances in Manchester, Liverpool and Birmingham. It was with a feeling of pride and fulfilment that Elizabeth read the glowing reviews in the press. Gio's name was now made and, she was certain, he would go on to even greater things.

What a miracle, she continually reminded herself, that this boy should have been rescued from an early grave thanks to the efforts of Dr. Weissman. Within six months he had improved from a pale, pathetic invalid, with no hope of life, to a tanned, robust youth fit for anything. It seemed to her like the miracle of the century and she would continue to thank the doctor for the rest of her life. Already, with deep satisfaction, she had arranged to contribute regular donations to his funds.

As Gio's fees mounted up for his solo playing, he was able to offer Elizabeth the £12,000 purchase price for the violin. Though reluctant to accept it, she felt obliged to do so for Roger's sake. It was only fair that she should fulfil her part of the bargain of the running of Swallow Tree Gardens, and already the central heating had been delayed for over a year.

In the event Roger was in flippant mood on the day she confessed to him about the Italian violin. Instead of making a storm over it and, as she had feared, accusing her of deceit and incompetence, he replied sweetly:

'My dear Liz, nothing you do for music would ever surprise me! I believe you would go to the ends of the earth to satisfy your craving.'

Elizabeth blinked at him as he continued: 'If he's paying you back, tell him there's no hurry: let him enjoy himself first. After all, luv, how many people actually come back from the dead? That boy deserves something for his remarkable courage and I hope he gets it.'

The symphony also was just about complete. Peter had checked it through and made a few improvements. The whole thing was being submitted to the musical director of the London College of Music for his opinion.

By summer's end the manuscript had been passed around to several musicians and it was decided to try the symphony out at the Wigmore Hall, where most first performances are held, and that the London Symphony Orchestra should play it.

This trip to London was equally spectacular. Thrilled beyond words, Elizabeth surveyed the stage of the famed hall from her front row seat, with Gio sitting on one side of her and Roger on the other. Dr. and Mrs. Emmanual were in the row behind. The symphony sounded strange and unfamiliar but it was smooth flowing and full of feeling. Any first performance was always a strain, Elizabeth kept telling herself, both to the players and also to the audience. Most music lovers really preferred something they knew, and other work required special concentration and an open mind.

She watched Gio's face without appearing to do so. He wouldn't have known anyway: he was obviously transported into another world for the whole forty minutes. As composer, he was called on to the stage at the end of the symphony, and this was his moment of real triumph as he came down from the stage to loud continued applause. The adulation did not go to his head, Elizabeth observed. He never appeared conceited or superior, but was still her Gio, the same boy she had taken into her house a year and a half ago.

Peter was just as anxious for Gio to get on. As soon as his health allowed, he enrolled him at the Conservatoire at Leningrad and entered him for the Tchaikovsky Competition: 'He stands as good a chance as any other solo player, Liz, and somebody gets the prize every year. He aims now to learn five or six concertos from memory, and then he will be in a position to do a world tour. We shan't be seeing much of Giovanni in this town, I'm afraid.'

'Yes, that's the trouble.' Elizabeth was doing her level best to be sensible. 'It's the awful part. You help them on, and then you have to know when to let go. One thing, he's got his health back. And these successes are a bonus, I suppose.'

'Well, it's all thanks to you, Liz. Without you Gio wouldn't have been with us at all.'

He gave her a warm smile and a wave of joy swept through her as he showered on her one of his rare compliments.

Why did this boy make such a difference to her life, she pondered? Ever since he had come along her whole attitude to life seemed to have changed. Suddenly she found herself with something to live for. Had not Roger told her, 'Liz, m'dear, there's a certain radiance about your face which I haven't seen for years'? It was that feeling of exhilaration and fulfilment that had put the impetus back into her life and re-kindled her love for Roger. Gio's arrival had undoubtedly sparked this off and now Roger and she had found each other again . . . wonder of wonders.

How had she managed so long without loving him? It was mad to have pushed him away from her six years ago and try to manage on her own. She might be a good organiser but still she needed a man. Losing little Tim must have played upon her mind. They had drifted apart until they were almost like strangers, their conversations just on the surface. That night Roger came home unexpectedly to find Gio occupying his room, he must have felt pangs of jealousy, and that was why he had gone and got drunk. So he must have thought a bit about her then. What a good thing she had known how to deal with him and kept calm for Gio's sake. It had turned out for the best in the end, and now Roger admired the boy for what he was. Had he not remarked only yesterday: 'Gosh, I'd give anything to have Gio's mentality and alertness!'

Roger had been a good husband really, and so understanding and forgiving. All the time she neglected him, he had been there on the sidelines, waiting for her to come to her senses.

The following day Roger read out the headlines in the *Weekly News* about Idris Jones' arrest.

'Just listen to this, Liz, what you've been waiting for, I should think! 'Like Father Like Son', it says here. And then: 'Idris Jones, aged twenty-five, has been convicted of smuggling cannabis and hiding it in an out-building on his smallholding. His father Zechariah was convicted fifteen years ago of fraudulent dealings in penicillin and anti-biotics, and struck off the Register of Veterinary Surgeons.'

'What a good thing it's come to light,' Elizabeth said quietly. 'They're both such a rotten example to the community that nothing in their past would surprise me.'

Roger was just as vehement: 'To think we've put up with their behaviour on the Town Council all this time. Now they'll be moving out of the area in disgrace and, if the judge has any sense, Idris will get a spell inside. This is the best piece of news I've heard in a long time, and I know how pleased Peter and the "friends of the orchestra" will be.'

More good news came the same day: a letter for Peter from the Education Department to say that his interview at Caernarvon had been successful. The new music section at the college would open in October and Peter, appointed Head of Department, would be able to choose his own tutors and arrange his own syllabus.

Glorious news indeed for the Palm Court Orchestra. They would arrive at Easter as usual, but this time with the added incentive of jobs for them during the following winter and spring. It would in fact be full-time work on a permanent basis, and a Student's Orchestra would be formed to give concerts all the year round.

Sylvia and Martin, now married, looked a picture of happiness. They had taken a flat for a few weeks whilst they looked for the right house. So deliriously happy did Sylvia look that Elizabeth would not have been surprised to hear of a baby on the way.

The Season started with a bang and the first concert at the pier head held extra attractions. Roger had had the whole pavilion re-wired and put rows of fairy lights at the entrance and all round the cafe. He had also flood-lit the building brilliantly, so that, from the mainland, it looked like a fairy-tale castle out at sea.

Peter had arranged for the best children's choir to come along and give the season a lively start, and the 'friends' had canvassed the area and promised free coffee and scones in the interval.

Elizabeth still took her place in the front row to listen to the Palm Court Orchestra. It was still her favourite orchestra, even without Gio there. As she sat, carried away into her special world of fantasy, she recalled how Gio had confided to her his innermost thoughts that night in her lounge. At the time it had seemed to her like an impossible dream, the indulgence of an over-imaginative schoolboy. Well in spite of everything, he had actually played his concerto, and his symphony had been performed and accepted. He possessed an authentic Italian violin such as he had always dreamed about and used it to give pleasure to many.

She would never forget his eager expression as he had related his life story to her: the good and the bad, the light and the shade. His hopes, dreams and fears . . . And now, with all three ambitions achieved, he was still the same Gio. He had taught her so much about life and music, and everything that really matttered in life. His influence would always be there, in her house, even if he were on the other side of the world. Most important of all, his child would be there and she would be caring for it. There was nothing on earth that she could wish for more than that.

Chapter 18

'Dear Mrs. Williams, My baby is beautiful. My head it is all mixed up and my heart is breaking. A lot there is to say now. Please come and talk. Love Gretta.'

Elizabeth's heart gave a curious lurch and she felt numb with shock as she passed the unwelcome letter to Roger, who was fussing around the kitchen collecting up his fishing tackle.

'Didn't I say it was all going too easily?' he demanded. 'Bound to be a hitch or two on the way. People have feelings and emotions they cannot always control.'

'But how could Gretta possibly change her mind after all these months?' wailed Elizabeth. 'She doesn't really want the baby. Her career is involved, her parents, her whole life . . .'

'Relax now, Liz. It isn't the end, you know. We can even wait for our own child if all this comes to nothing.'

It was half an hour's ride to Bangor Maternity. Elizabeth's heart thumped and she felt churned up inside as she manoeuvred her car through the traffic, overtaking whenever she could in order to reach Gretta's bedside in double quick time.

Whatever could the girl mean? Only one thing, that she wanted to keep the baby. The baby she herself had longed for all these months, and which had come to mean everything to her. She must talk to the girl, woman to woman. Gretta was no longer a child, but had a woman's instincts and emotions, and this maternal emotion which must have gripped her might not easily be stifled. This was indeed a knotty problem which she really should not have overlooked.

Life ahead, it seemed, was going to be desolate again. Gretta would take her baby home with her, and Gio would go far away to the famous Conservatoire of Leningrad to continue his studies. Luckily Roger — dear kind Roger — would always be there. What a perfect gem he was — putting up with her demands, fitting in with her schemes, agreeing to her every whim.

Perhaps if she waited like other women there would be a baby for them and this would be another Timothy. Yes, she must settle for that. At least she loved Roger now and he loved her, and that was, or should be, the most important thing in her life. Why, oh why did she have to be different? It was this music thing every time. She felt devastated.

Hospital rules permitted no visitors except mother or husband for the first ten days, so Elizabeth had not yet seen the baby, Frau Deutchtung having taken over. But a wonderful sensation had rushed through her veins, like red wine at a party, when the news had come through of the birth of a baby girl weighing seven pounds, with mother and child doing well. Oblivious to Gretta's feelings, Elizabeth had experienced nothing but joy for herself at the thought that Gio's child would soon be hers. So obsessed had she become with the fulfilment of all her dreams that it had never occurred to her that Gretta might have second thoughts.

Walking the length of the hospital corridor, she approached Gretta's bed with a forced smile and an artificial cheerfulness.

'How good it is to see you looking so bright! Tell me just how you feel.'

She kissed the girl's flushed cheek, taking one of her soft white hands to squeeze it affectionately.

'Oh, Mrs. Williams, I am full of love for my little one. She is mine — she cannot be anyone else's.'

Elizabeth sat down beside the bed, seeking the right words.

'If that's how you feel, Gretta, there is very little I can say. But remember you have your career at stake. You had big ideas and so did your parents. And what about all your friends at home? They will be greatly shocked when they know.'

Resourceful as ever, she was playing every card in the pack. There must be some way of changing this girl's mind. She didn't even wish to see the baby if it wasn't hers. It was a horrible thought, but that was how she felt.

'The baby is part of me, you see. Like myself I love her, this little precious one — how can I part with her?'

Gretta's mind seemed to be made up. She went on that the

sight of other mothers in the ward had given her a different outlook: mothers with happiness written all over their faces. It was a feeling which had to be experienced to be believed and she felt fulfilled and happy at the prospect of motherhood.

The girl did indeed look radiant and her eyes shone with a newfound wonderment. With a quick farewell and a kiss, Elizabeth turned swiftly from the bed and, walking out of the ward, burst into tears.

*   *   *   *

The following day there was a surprise visitor to Swallow Tree Gardens. Elizabeth had not seen Gwyneth Jones since her visit to the smallholding, so she was astonished to see the woman knocking on her back door as timidly as a small boy stealing apples from an orchard.

'Mrs. Williams,' she faltered as Elizabeth opened the door, 'I apologise for coming round the back; I didn't want to bother you at the front door in case you were in the kitchen . . . '

'It's nice to see you, Gwyneth, after all this time. Do come inside. I'll put the kettle on.'

In the middle of a pile of ironing, she switched off the iron, ushered Gwyneth into the lounge and showed her to a seat.

'Staying with my sister, I am,' volunteered Gwyneth after an awkward silence. 'You are the person I can talk to more than anyone else, Mrs. Williams. You were so kind when you came to see me, with not one word against my Idris. I don't forget such things.'

Placing a dainty tray on a side table, Elizabeth poured out two cups and handed one to Gwyneth, with a selection of fancy cakes. The woman sat on the extreme edge of her chair and, taking two lumps of sugar, stirred her tea in a dreamy fashion. She was obviously wearing her sister's clothes, the skirt and coat two or three inches too long for her. Her lank brown hair needed a trim and her lack of make-up gave her an even plainer appearance.

'How is Zechariah, Gwyneth? And have you heard anything from Idris?'

Elizabeth tried to sound cheerful. It was difficult to know how to start a conversation under such circumstances.

'Left him I did. Awful it was living with him, what with Idris

137

being sent to Walton jail. A filthy temper Zech has . . . It went to his head when he read all about himself in the paper. Got quite violent, he did, so I made up my mind and left.'

Elizabeth looked kindly at the woman: 'Well, Gwyneth, that's all in the past now and you must look to the future. Are you able to visit Idris from time to time?'

'Oh yes, I go once a fortnight and take him chocolates and cigarettes and papers. Lucky he was to get only three years. Could be out in two if he behaves.'

There was another awkward silence, with Elizabeth feeling quite out of her depth. She could not remember any conversation like this ever before.

Finally Gwyneth resumed in a subdued tone: 'It is work I want now, Mrs. Williams. Do you by any chance know of anyone who'd take me on? I'm not one of yer fancy women, too proud to go down on their hands and knees. No, I'm quite prepared to clean anybody's lavatory for them and see to the drains.'

Poor Gwyneth sounded quite desperate. Elizabeth felt nothing but pity for her as she continued:

'My sister says I can stay for a week or two, but I'm not one to impose. It's work I want. I'd feel more at home doing hotel work like I used to before Zech came along. Rough work is all right with me — just anything, in fact.'

Having got that off her chest, Gwyneth took a large bite out of a slice of chocolate gateau, smacking her lips with relish, then washed it down with a gulp of tea. Elizabeth poured her another cup, then smiled graciously into Gwyneth's brown eyes. This woman had looked her up because she considered she was kind and understanding. She must try and live up to her reputation. Gwyneth had the courage to return to the town where her husband and son had disgraced themselves, and was prepared to take on any job she could get hold of. Surely it was up to her to help out all she could.

'As a matter of fact, Gwyneth, I can do with someone here for the season. It's only temporary work, you understand, but there's all the upstairs work for the visitors, the washing-up and the cleaning.'

Gwyneth's face lit up as she spoke. The tinge of colour which came into her sallow cheeks made her look almost pretty.

'I've an attic room you can use for sleeping but if you want to be independent I know a friend who will let you have a

138

flatlet for the summer. With your wages and tips you would be able to pay your way.'

As she let Gwyneth out half-an-hour later, and watched her slim figure disappear into the shadows, Elizabeth felt in her heart that she had done the right thing.

But that same heart was full of anguish when she recalled her conversation with Gretta the previous day. The baby so long awaited was not after all to be hers. Life then, to Elizabeth, looked very grim indeed.

Chapter 19

The situation changed dramatically in a few hours, with a phone call from Gretta's father. In perfect English, he was able to tell Elizabeth the whole story.

He had arrived at the hospital soon after she had left. His other daughter, Tanzi, had come along, fresh and youthful, bubbling over with fun. Overjoyed to see one another, the sisters had embraced each other in the hospital ward.

Ignoring Gretta's talk about keeping the baby, her father had put forward his scheme. Having found her a place in Munich University, to commence at end of May, he promised her a new car and a course of driving lessons if she did well in her first term. Tanzi had talked excitedly about the new ski-ing gear their father had bought for the girls and the ski-tuition he had arranged for them in the Alps next month. A trip to Paris in the summer, with new clothes for both of them from a famous boutique, was another treat in store.

All in all, Herr Deutchtung had displayed a certain subtlety, involving his daughters in such a round of activity that having a baby to carry around would be nothing but an added complication. Enveloped in such enthusiasm, Gretta's mind had switched automatically back to the happy carefree life she had enjoyed before coming to North Wales. It was the easiest thing in the world for her emotions to change gear again and accept the inevitable idea of parting with her baby. Far better to return home with her father and sister, take up the threads where she had left off and start all over again. The spasm of heartache over the baby would soon pass. After all, not many girls of her age could look forward to a ski-ing holiday and a car all in the same year. Obviously her father understood just how she felt and was trying to make up for the agony of mind she had been going through. Elizabeth had been right all along: she must leave her baby behind and forget all about her. From now on her life would be unfettered and free.

*   *   *   *

The clock in the lounge said just after four o'clock, the time for the afternoon feed. Elizabeth adjusted her left arm to make the infant more comfortable, her other hand holding the bottle half full of warm sweet milk. She had 'winded' the baby in the accepted way, holding its body across her shoulder and giving it a firm but gentle pat on the back. Now she was careful to control the flow of milk as it disappeared miraculously from the plastic bottle. The familiar smells of talcum powder and baby food permeated the room, and the soft petal skin of the body nestling against hers was like nectar and ambrosia all rolled into one.

What a contented baby she was, sucking eagerly to drain the very last drop of warm liquid from the bottle. Elizabeth was encouraged by the sure knowledge that she still had the 'mother touch' and the special skill necessary in handling such a small child. As she gazed at the clear-cut features of the small pink face, with its big black eyes and flecks of dark hair appearing in wavelets all over the head, Elizabeth's cup of happiness was full to overflowing. She could once more bask in the role of motherhood, a vocation which had eluded her all these years.

She surveyed the line of washing across her lawn — spotless white terylene squares, pink matinee jackets, hand-knitted vests. You've always had this maternal instinct, she reminded herself. Wasn't that what you felt about Gio? It's something that can't be quenched and, when fulfilled, is absolute bliss.

In three weeks time the legal formalities would be complete. The baby would be theirs, hers and Roger's, in every sense of the word, with a birth certificate bearing their names and no mention of any other names at all.

Gretta had finally handed over the baby with a look of relief and gratitude. Gratitude, Elizabeth thought, because she knew her baby was dropping into a good home; relief that the awful ordeal was over. In all probability they would never meet again. Herr Deutchtung had certainly played his cards well.

Typically, Roger had taken the matter in his stride. If his wife was happy so was he. Always, he assured her, he had wished for a girl. He turned out to be a source of strength in every way, as keen as she was in the matter of choosing names.

'What about Rhiannon, Liz? I've always liked that.'

Roger looked proudly at his baby daughter and beamed with pleasure as he detected, or so he thought, a tiny smile on her face.

'Yes, Rhiannon sounds all right. And I like Glenda. We could have them both.'

'Rhiannon Glenda Williams,' he repeated. 'Who could improve on that?'

Elizabeth held the baby closely. The bottle now finished, the tiny eyes were closing in sleep. Everything had worked out perfectly, she pondered. How lucky she had been to get hold of Blodwen from a village near Llanberis. A strong, healthy, out-door type, she was happy to leave that quiet, desolate area and join the bright lights of the summer season at the seaside resort. Having taken her degree in nursery nursing, she loved children, and particularly babies, and could safely be trusted to look after Rhiannon while Elizabeth herself was engaged with the visitors. She might even be able to attend some of the concerts if Blodwen would take over during the evenings. Gwyneth too had come along just at the right time, and could be depended upon for all the rough work.

Happiness flowed through Elizabeth's veins like wine and this warm feeling stole again over her heart as she gazed at the small oval face now peaceful in sleep. A tiny life just beginning, she reflected, clinging and helpless, dependent entirely on her and Roger, and theirs for keeps.

The ten o'clock feed came and went and Rhiannon was settled for the night in her pink and white cot upstairs. Then Elizabeth joined Roger in one of the comfortable easy chairs in her private lounge. She was seeing far more of him these days, and prone to snuggle up close to him like they used to years ago.

'You know, Roger,' she murmured, 'it all seems too good to be true. Life isn't usually so easy, is it? The ends don't always tie up as neatly as they've done for us.'

'We've been lucky, luv.'

As Roger flicked through the records, trying to find one of his favourites, Elizabeth stared pensively at the ceiling.

'Only Peter knows where our baby came from. As far as I

know the news hasn't leaked out; we were careful not to talk too much about it, and the people around here think we dealt with an adoption society.'

'That's all right then.'

'And yet, Roger, I feel frightened that something is going to happen. It's all turned out too perfect to be real — I can't help feeling a bit scared.'

And Elizabeth was right.

Chapter 20

A week later Swallow Tree Gardens had a visitor, none other than Vic Simpson, Gio's favourite tutor, the one he had talked so much about.

Elizabeth had almost forgotten Vic Simpson. She had often felt pangs of jealousy when she realised that Vic had been prominent in Gio's life and helped to mould his character long before she knew him. Gio would have confided in his tutor all his confidences, his daydreams and his ambitions, just as he had done with her. Hadn't he turned up at the crucial moment when Gio was expected to die and moved heaven and earth to gain as much detail as he could of the boy's lifestyle? So it was with complete surprise that Elizabeth opened her front door to this man thrusting a brown paper parcel into her arms.

'My book is now complete, Mrs. Williams. Giovanni's life story, set out in these pages. Allow me to have the pleasure . . .'

'Come inside, Mr. Simpson. So your book is actually completed after all this time. I thought seeing Gio had recovered, you would have abandoned the idea . . .'

'Oh no, I carried on just the same. But the fact that he is still alive does of course take away all the drama. Nobody wants to hear of the successes of the living. You have to die before you are famous, particularly in the world of music.'

'Oh come now, Mr. Simpson! Gio is famous already, or am I prejudiced? Do you prefer tea or sherry?'

Ushering him into her lounge, she opened up the cocktail cabinet while Vic took the brown paper from his parcel and handed the manuscript to her.

Elizabeth scanned the typed pages, assimilating as much as she could. The matter was well written and all rang true. The

144

man had gone to great lengths to portray as much of Gio's life as he knew about, including the orphanage, the college of music, Swallow Tree Gardens, the clinic and then his recent successes. There was a certain brilliance about the style which surprised her.

As Elizabeth read, Vic drained his sherry glass and went to stand by the patio window, surveying her line of washing blowing about in the wind.

Finally she commenced: 'It's a good record of the boy's life. When do you expect to get it published?'

Enjoying her own sherry, she poured Vic a second glass. There was an impression of uneasiness about his habit of striding about the room and not meeting her gaze.

'So glad you like the results.' His tone was oily now. 'There is one chapter not there, Mrs. Williams, and that is where you come in. My book is very detailed,with information gleaned from every possible source. Did you know that I went to Geneva? No? I followed Giovanni about like a reporter would follow a celebrity. There is nothing left out: absolutely nothing. The last chapter is more — revealing, shall we say? It is the matter of Gio's child . . . Your baby to be precise!'

Elizabeth's heart dropped like a stone. How on earth did Vic know about the baby? They had told not a single living soul, apart from Peter as Gio's guardian.

'I don't know what you mean,' she shrieked. 'What conncetion has my baby to do with your book?'

Staring at him in horror, she noted a gleam of satisfaction in his eyes — as if he was enjoying her humiliation.

'Don't panic, lady, all is not lost. You know as well as I do that those nappies flapping in the wind have as much to do with this book as the other information it contains. If you want me to withhold the last chapter you have only to do as I say.'

Elizabeth's mouth became dry and when she tried to speak nothing came.

'I've tried every publisher around,' continued Vic. 'The climate is bad and I've come up against a brick wall. I happen to know one of those publishers who will print at the author's expense, so what I require, here and now, is the simple sum of £6,000 to finance the publication of 2,000 copies. A large number of these copies will be yours within six months, Mrs. Williams. And the final chapter to which I refer will be scrapped.'

Elizabeth's eyes flashed. 'How dare you, Mr. Simpson!' Her tone was high pitched now. 'I'll get my husband and my solicitor. What you are saying is nothing short of blackmail. Kindly leave my house at once, and take your manuscript with you.'

Boiling with rage, she almost pushed Vic Simpson through the front door.

It was a comfort to her to hear Roger arriving back from his trip and opening the door into the kitchen. What a relief to be able to unburden herself and tell him the whole story. He listened carefully as it all came tumbling out.

'Not to worry, Liz, there's sure to be a way out,' he drawled reassuringly. 'Such a man as that can never succeed. Tell you what, why not talk it over with Peter? If, as you say, he knows this chap well, he may think of a way to shut him up. I'll take over here while you toddle off.'

Peter and Elizabeth sat opposite each other in his lounge, the soft light of the fire adding charm to an already beguiling room. As Elizabeth repeated Vic Simpson's story word for word Peter's eyes widened and he sank deeper into his comfortable chair, puffing lazily at his cigar.

'Well, well, well . . .' He whistled: 'To think of Vic Simpson resorting to blackmail! He's always been short of money, but a mean trick such as this . . .' The doctor shook his head.

'How on *earth* did he find out? We've all been so meticulously careful.'

'Never mind that. The fact is he does know — and, my dear, I think *I* know of a way out. The picture isn't by any means as black as it looks. You say he's staying at the Mountain View? I'll pop along there tonight to give that young man a piece of my mind.'

*　　*　　*　　*

It was midnight when the door bell rang. Elizabeth almost cried out in delight as she saw Peter there. The very fact that he was smiling must surely be a good omen?

'Nothing to drink, thank you,' he assured her. 'I had plenty of that at the Mountain View. Would you believe I was there for two hours?'

'Do sit down, Peter, and I'll call Roger.' She switched on the electric fire and drew three chairs around it.

146

'It's a long story but I felt I must come along and tell you, otherwise I couldn't imagine you getting much sleep. I doubt if you'll see Vic Simpson in this area again.'

Peter looked complacent, clearly enjoying the build-up to his story. If only he would get to the point!

Seeing Elizabeth's imploring look, he went on, 'You remember, Liz, how when you took music exams on the piano, you would enter the exam room, play your pieces and scales in front of the examiner, and then go off home and wait for the results by post?'

'Yes, of course. I should do, I took seven of the wretched things! What has that to do with Vic?'

'There's a loophole in the rules. The Associated Board haven't been made aware of it. If you remember, Liz, there was no proof, when you played your pieces, that you were the person supposed to be taking the exam. You could have been anyone: it was the way the pieces were played that mattered. Vic had a pupil who was desperately keen to get into college. He just had to get through his Grade VII, but he hadn't the nerve for it. Vic substituted another student who passed with merit, and so the boy went to college although it was fraud. Actually the boy left college the following year, as he was unsuited to it, and I know exactly where he is. He would make a good witness. I can expose Vic if necessary, and I told him so. Then there was the matter of the City and Guild Examination Papers. Vic stole them overnight and took copies of the questions. I have evidence and witnesses and would reveal everything to the authorities if need be.'

Elizabeth could have danced for joy round the room. Instead she remained seated, glancing wonderingly from Peter to Roger.

'But what did you do about it? How on earth did he react? If only I could have been there to see the wretch's face!'

'It's a most serious offence, which could mean his job. If this was exposed Vic Simpson would never hold his head up in public again.'

'So you threatened him, I take it?'

'I did more than that — I made him sell me the manuscript for £1,000! I knew you would share it with me. A private publisher friend of mine will print 150 copies for us for the modest sum of £700 and we can sell them to the Friends of the Orchestra for a fiver each. In that way we'll get all the cash back. Do you know, Liz, Vic was really fed-up with his book and glad enough to be

147

of it in the end. He would rather Gio had died: then it would have been a goldmine for him.'

'Are you sure he won't come back, Peter,' Roger added, 'to make more trouble?'

'Most unlikely when he went off with his tail so very much between his legs. He had no idea I had so much knowledge of his past life. You should have seen how scared he looked when I brought out all the gen. about his fraudulent practices. I really put the fear of God into him!'

* * * *

Elizabeth and Roger had spent more time together since the baby had come. Rhiannon, a bond they shared, had done so much to bring them even closer.

The strangest thing about it all, mused Elizabeth, was the fact that Gio never knew he was responsible.

She mentioned this to Roger: 'Isn't it amazing, darling, how naive Gio is in such matters? He'll never know he is the father of little Rhiannon. Didn't it fit in well, he being in the clinic all the time Gretta was having the baby?'

'We wouldn't want him to know, luv,' Roger remarked. 'And he wouldn't welcome it. Not that type at all, y'know — he'd never conform to a mundane type of family life.'

Elizabeth slid an arm round Roger's waist, her other arm supporting the child.

'This is our baby, Roger . . .our own wonderful secret. Nobody will find out now. Rhiannon Glenda is ours, yours and mine.'

She realised then, to the full, that nothing could be better than the three of them living at Swallow Tree Gardens. There would always be music in her home and from now on, she and Roger would enjoy a perfect family life together. Her cup of happiness was indeed filled to overflowing.

THE END